COLLECTED WORKS OF
ARNOLD BENNETT

CONTENTS

THE AUTHOR'S CRAFT

LITERARY TASTE

THE FEAST OF ST. FRIEND

THE AUTHOR'S CRAFT

* * * * *

PART I.

SEEING LIFE

I

A young dog, inexperienced, sadly lacking in even primary education, ambles and frisks along the footpath of Fulham Road, near the mysterious gates of a Marist convent. He is a large puppy, on the way to be a dog of much dignity, but at present he has little to recommend him but that gawky elegance, and that bounding gratitude for the gift of life, which distinguish the normal puppy. He is an ignorant fool. He might have entered the convent of nuns and had a fine time, but instead he steps off the pavement into the road, the road being a vast and interesting continent imperfectly explored. His confidence in his nose, in his agility, and in the goodness of God is touching, absolutely painful to witness. He glances casually at a huge, towering vermilion construction that is whizzing towards him on four wheels, preceded by a glint of brass and a wisp of steam; and then with disdain he ignores it as less important than a mere speck of odorous matter in the mud. The next instant he is lying inert in the mud. His confidence in the goodness of God had been misplaced. Since the beginning of time God had ordained him a victim.

An impressive thing happens. The motor-bus reluctantly slackens and stops. Not the differential brake, nor the foot-brake, has arrested the motor-bus, but the invisible brake of public opinion, acting by administrative

11

transmission. There is not a policeman in sight. Theoretically, the motor-'bus is free to whiz onward in its flight to the paradise of Shoreditch, but in practice it is paralysed by dread. A man in brass buttons and a stylish cap leaps down from it, and the blackened demon who sits on its neck also leaps down from it, and they move gingerly towards the puppy. A little while ago the motor-bus might have overturned a human cyclist or so, and proceeded nonchalant on its way. But now even a puppy requires a post-mortem: such is the force of public opinion aroused. Two policemen appear in the distance.

"A street accident" is now in being, and a crowd gathers with calm joy and stares, passive and determined. The puppy offers no sign whatever; just lies in the road. Then a boy, destined probably to a great future by reason of his singular faculty of initiative, goes to the puppy and carries him by the scruff of the neck, to the shelter of the gutter. Relinquished by the boy, the lithe puppy falls into an easy horizontal attitude, and seems bent upon repose. The boy lifts the puppy's head to examine it, and the head drops back wearily. The puppy is dead. No cry, no blood, no disfigurement! Even no perceptible jolt of the wheel as it climbed over the obstacle of the puppy's body! A wonderfully clean and perfect accident!

The increasing crowd stares with beatific placidity. People emerge impatiently from the bowels of the throbbing motor-bus and slip down from its back, and either join the crowd or vanish. The two policemen and the crew of the motor-bus have now met in parley. The conductor and the driver have an air at once nervous and resigned; their gestures are quick and vivacious. The policemen, on the other hand, indicate by their slow and huge movements that eternity is theirs. And they could not be more sure of the conductor and the driver if they had them manacled and leashed. The conductor and the driver admit the absolute dominion of the elephantine policemen; they admit that before the simple will of the policemen inconvenience, lost minutes, shortened leisure, docked wages, count as less than naught. And the policemen are carelessly sublime, well knowing that magistrates, jails, and the very Home Secretary on his throne—yes, and a whole system of conspiracy and perjury and brutality—are at their beck in case of need. And yet occasionally in the demeanour of the policemen towards the conductor and the driver there is a silent message that says: "After all, we, too, are working men like you, over-worked and under-paid and bursting with grievances in the service of the pitiless and dishonest public. We, too, have wives and children and privations and frightful apprehensions. We, too, have to struggle desperately. Only the awful magic of these garments and of the garter which we wear on our wrists sets an abyss between us and you." And the conductor writes and one of the policemen writes, and they keep on writing, while the traffic makes beautiful curves to avoid them.

The still increasing crowd continues to stare in the pure blankness of pleasure. A close-shaved, well-dressed, middle-aged man, with a copy of *The Sportsman* in his podgy hand, who has descended from the motor-bus, starts stamping his feet. "I was knocked down by a taxi last year," he says fiercely. "But nobody took no notice of *that*! Are they going to stop here all the blank morning for a blank tyke?" And for all his respectable appearance, his features become debased, and he emits a jet of disgusting profanity and brings most of the Trinity into the thunderous assertion that he has paid his fare. Then a man passes wheeling a muck-cart. And he stops and talks a long time with the other uniforms, because he, too, wears vestiges of a uniform. And the crowd never moves nor ceases to stare. Then the new arrival stoops and picks up the unclaimed, masterless puppy, and flings it, all soft and yielding, into the horrid mess of the cart, and passes on. And only that which is immortal and divine of the puppy remains behind, floating perhaps like an invisible vapour over the scene of the tragedy.

The crowd is tireless, all eyes. The four principals still converse and write. Nobody in the crowd comprehends what they are about. At length the driver separates himself, but is drawn back, and a new parley is commenced. But everything ends. The policemen turn on their immense heels. The driver and conductor race towards the motor-bus.

The bell rings, the motor-bus, quite empty, disappears snorting round the corner into Walham Green. The crowd is now lessening. But it separates with reluctance, many of its members continuing to stare with intense absorption at the place where the puppy lay or the place where the policemen stood. An appreciable interval elapses before the "street accident" has entirely ceased to exist as a phenomenon.

The members of the crowd follow their noses, and during the course of the day remark to acquaintances:

"Saw a dog run over by a motor-bus in the Fulham Road this morning! Killed dead!"

And that is all they do remark. That is all they have witnessed. They will not, and could not, give intelligible and in teresting particulars of the affair (unless it were as to the breed of the dog or the number of the bus-service). They have watched a dog run over. They analyse neither their sensations nor the phenomenon. They have witnessed it whole, as a bad writer uses a *cliché*. They have observed—that is to say, they have really seen—nothing.

* * * * *

II

It will be well for us not to assume an attitude of condescension towards the crowd. Because in the matter of looking without seeing we are all about equal. We all go to and fro in a state of the observing faculties which somewhat resembles coma. We are all content to look and not see.

And if and when, having comprehended that the *rôle* of observer is not passive but active, we determine by an effort to rouse ourselves from the coma and really to see the spectacle of the world (a spectacle surpassing circuses and even street accidents in sustained dramatic interest), we shall discover, slowly in the course of time, that the act of seeing, which seems so easy, is not so easy as it seems. Let a man resolve: "I will keep my eyes open on the way to the office of a morning," and the probability if that for many mornings he will see naught that is not trivial, and that his system of perspective will be absurdly distorted. The unusual, the unaccustomed, will infallibly attract him, to the exclusion of what is fundamental and universal. Travel makes observers of us all, but the things which as travellers we observe generally show how unskilled we are in the new activity.

A man went to Paris for the first time, and observed right off that the carriages of suburban trains had seats on the roof like a tramcar. He was so thrilled by the remarkable discovery that he observed almost nothing else. This enormous fact occupied the whole foreground of his perspective. He returned home and announced that Paris was a place where people rode on the tops of trains. A Frenchwoman came to London for the first time—and no English person would ever guess the phenomenon which vanquished all others in her mind on the opening day. She saw a cat walking across a street. The vision excited her. For in Paris cats do not roam in thoroughfares, because there are practically no houses with gardens or "areas"; the flat system is unfavourable to the enlargement of cats. I remember once, in the days when observation had first presented itself to me as a beautiful pastime, getting up very early and making the circuit of inner London before summer dawn in quest of interesting material. And the one note I gathered was that the ground in front of the all-night coffee-stalls was white with egg-shells! What I needed then was an operation for cataract. I also remember taking a man to the opera who had never seen an opera. The work was *Lohengrin*. When we came out he said: "That swan's neck was rather stiff." And it was all he did say. We went and had a drink. He was not mistaken. His observation was most just; but his perspective was that of those literary critics who give ten lines to point ing out three slips of syntax, and three lines to an ungrammatical admission that the novel under survey is not wholly tedious.

But a man may acquire the ability to observe even a large number of facts, and still remain in the infantile stage of observation. I have read, in some work of literary criticism, that Dickens could walk up one side of a long, busy street and down the other, and then tell you in their order the names on all the shop-signs; the fact was alleged as an illustration of his great powers of observation. Dickens was a great observer, but he would assuredly have been a still greater observer had he been a little less pre-occupied with trivial and unco-ordinated details. Good observation consists not in multiplicity of detail, but in co-ordination of detail according to a true perspective of relative importance, so that a finally just general impression may be reached in the shortest possible time. The skilled observer is he who does not have to change his mind. One has only to compare one's present adjusted impression of an intimate friend with one's first impression of him to perceive the astounding inadequacy of one's powers of observation. The man as one has learnt to see him is simply not the same man who walked into one's drawing-room on the day of introduction.

There are, by the way, three sorts of created beings who are sentimentally supposed to be able to judge individuals at the first glance: women, children, and dogs. By virtue of a mystic gift with which rumour credits them, they are never mistaken. It is merely not true. Women are constantly quite wrong in the estimates based on their "feminine instinct"; they sometimes even admit it; and the matrimonial courts prove it *passim*. Children are more often wrong than women. And as for dogs, it is notorious that they are for ever being taken in by plausible scoundrels; the perspective of dogs is grotesque. Not seldom have I grimly watched the gradual disillusion of deceived dogs. Nevertheless, the sentimental legend of the infallibility of women, children, and dogs, will persist in Anglo-Saxon countries.

* * * * *

III

One is curious about one's fellow-creatures: therefore one watches them. And generally the more intelligent one is, the more curious one is, and the more one observes. The mere satisfaction of this curiosity is in itself a worthy end, and would alone justify the business of systematised observation. But the aim of observation may, and should, be expressed in terms more grandiose. Human curiosity counts among the highest social virtues (as indifference counts among the basest defects), because it leads to the disclosure of the causes of character and temperament and thereby to a better understanding of the springs of human conduct. Observation is not practised directly with this high end in view (save by prigs and other futile souls); nevertheless it is a moral act and must inevitably promote kindliness—whether we like it or not. It also sharpens the sense of beauty. An ugly deed—such as a deed of cruelty—takes on artistic beauty when its origin and hence its fitness in the general scheme begin to be comprehended. In the perspective of history we can derive an æsthetic pleasure from the tranquil scrutiny of all kinds of conduct—as well, for example, of a Renaissance Pope as of a Savonarola. Observation endows our day and our street with the romantic charm of history, and stimulates charity—not the charity which signs cheques, but the more precious charity which puts itself to the trouble of understanding. The one condition is that the observer must never lose sight of the fact that what he is trying to see is life, is the woman next door, is the man in the train—and not a concourse of abstractions. To appreciate all this is the first inspiring preliminary to sound observation.

* * * * *

IV

The second preliminary is to realise that all physical phenomena are interrelated, that there is nothing which does not bear on everything else. The whole spectacular and sensual show—what the eye sees, the ear hears, the nose scents, the tongue tastes and the skin touches—is a cause or an effect of human conduct. Naught can be ruled out as negligible, as not forming part of the equation. Hence he who would beyond all others see life for himself—I naturally mean the novelist and playwright—ought to embrace all phenomena in his curiosity. Being finite, he cannot. Of course he cannot! But he can, by obtaining a broad notion of the whole, determine with some accuracy the position and relative importance of the particular series of phenomena to which his instinct draws him. If he does not thus envisage the immense background of his special interests, he will lose the most precious feeling for interplay and proportion without which all specialism becomes distorted and positively darkened.

Now, the main factor in life on this planet is the planet itself. Any logically conceived survey of existence must begin with geographical and climatic phenomena. This is surely obvious. If you say that you are not interested in meteorology or the configurations of the earth, I say that you deceive yourself. You are. For an east wind may upset your liver and cause you to insult your wife. Beyond question the most important fact about, for example, Great Britain is that it is an island. We sail amid the Hebrides, and then talk of the fine qualities and the distressing limitations of those islanders; it ought to occur to us English that we are talking of ourselves in little. In moments of journalistic vainglory we are apt to refer to the "sturdy island race," meaning us. But that we are insular in the full significance of the horrid word is certain. Why not? A genuine observation of the supreme phenomenon that Great Britain is surrounded by water—an effort to keep it always at the back of the consciousness—will help to explain all the minor phenomena of British existence. Geographical knowledge is the mother of discernment, for the varying physical characteristics of the earth are the sole direct terrestrial influence determining the evolution of original vital energy.

All other influences are secondary, and have been effects of character and temperament before becoming causes. Perhaps the greatest of them are roads and architecture. Nothing could be more English than English roads, or more French than French roads. Enter England from France, let us say through the gate of Folkestone, and the architectural illustration which greets you (if you can look and see) is absolutely dramatic in its spectacular force. You say that there is no architecture in Folke stone. But Folkestone, like other towns, is just as full of architecture as a wood is full of trees. As the train winds on its causeway over the sloping town you perceive below you thousands of squat little homes, neat, tended, respectable, comfortable, prim, at once unostentatious and conceited. Each a separate, clearly-defined entity! Each saying to the others: "Don't look over my wall, and I won't look over yours!" Each with a ferocious jealousy bent on guarding its own individuality! Each a stronghold—an island! And all careless of the general effect, but making a very impressive general effect. The English race is below you. Your own son is below you insisting on the inviolability of his own den of a bedroom! . . . And contrast all that with the immense communistic and splendid façades of a French town, and work out the implications. If you really intend to see life you cannot afford to be blind to such thrilling phenomena.

Yet an inexperienced, unguided curiosity would be capable of walking through a French street and through an English street, and noting chiefly that whereas English lamp-posts spring from the kerb, French lamp-posts cling to the side of the house! Not that that detail is not worth noting. It is—in its place. French lamp-posts are part of what we call the "interesting character" of a French street. We say of a French street that it is "full of character." As if an English street was not! Such is blindness—to be cured by travel and the exercise of the logical faculty, most properly termed common sense. If one is struck by the magnificence of the great towns of the Continent, one should ratiocinate, and conclude that a major characteristic of the great towns of England is their shabby and higgledy-piggledy slovenliness. It is so. But there are people who have lived fifty years in Manchester, Leeds, Hull and Hanley without noticing it. The English idiosyncrasy is in that awful external slovenliness too, causing it, and being caused by it. Every street is a mirror, an illustration, an exposition, an explanation, of the human beings who live in it. Nothing in it is to be neglected. Everything in it is valuable, if the perspective is maintained. Nevertheless, in the narrow individualistic novels of English literature—and in some of the best—you will find a domestic organism described as though it existed in a vacuum, or in the Sahara, or between Heaven and earth; as though it reacted on nothing and was reacted on by nothing; and as though it could be adequately rendered without reference to anything exterior to itself. How can such novels satisfy a reader who has acquired or wants to acquire the faculty of seeing life?

* * * * *

V

The net result of the interplay of instincts and influences which determine the existence of a community is shown in the general expression on the faces of the people. This is an index which cannot lie and cannot be gainsaid. It is fairly easy, and extremely interesting, to decipher. It is so open, shameless, and universal, that not to look at it is impossible. Yet the majority of persons fail to see it. We hear of inquirers standing on London Bridge and counting the number of motor-buses, foot-passengers, lorries, and white horses that pass over the bridge in an hour. But we never hear of anybody counting the number of faces happy or unhappy, honest or rascally, shrewd or ingenuous, kind or cruel, that pass over the bridge. Perhaps the public may be surprised to hear that the general ex pression on the faces of Londoners of all ranks varies from the sad to the morose; and that their general mien is one of haste and gloomy preoccupation. Such a staring fact is paramount in sociological evidence. And the observer of it would be justified in summoning Heaven, the legislature, the county council, the churches, and the ruling classes, and saying to them: "Glance at these faces, and don't boast too much about what you have accomplished. The climate and the industrial system have so far triumphed over you all."

* * * * *

VI

When we come to the observing of the individual—to which all human observing does finally come if there is any right reason in it—the aforesaid general considerations ought to be ever present in the hinterland of the consciousness, aiding and influencing, perhaps vaguely, perhaps almost imperceptibly, the formation of judgments. If they do nothing else, they will at any rate accustom the observer to the highly important idea of the correlation of all phenomena. Especially in England a haphazard particularity is the chief vitiating element in the operations of the mind.

In estimating the individual we are apt not only to forget his environment, but—really strange!—to ignore much of the evidence visible in the individual himself. The inexperienced and ardent observer, will, for example, be astonishingly blind to everything in an individual except his face. Telling himself that the face must be the reflection of the soul, and that every thought and emotion leaves inevitably its mark there, he will concentrate on the face, singling it out as a phenomenon apart and self-complete. Were he a god and infallible, he could no doubt learn the whole truth from the face. But he is bound to fall into errors, and by limiting the field of vision he minimises the opportunity for correction. The face is, after all, quite a small part of the individual's physical organism. An Englishman will look at a woman's face and say she is a beautiful woman or a plain woman. But a woman may have a plain face, and yet by her form be entitled to be called beautiful, and (perhaps) *vice versâ*. It is true that the face is the reflexion of the soul. It is equally true that the carriage and gestures are the reflection of the soul. Had one eyes, the tying of a bootlace is the reflection of the soul. One piece of evidence can be used to correct every other piece of evidence. A refined face may be refuted by clumsy finger-ends; the eyes may contradict the voice; the gait may nullify the smile. None of the phenomena which every individual carelessly and brazenly displays in every motor-bus terrorising the streets of London is meaningless or negligible.

Again, in observing we are generally guilty of that particularity which results from sluggishness of the imagination. We may see the phenomenon at the moment of looking at it, but we particularise in that moment, making no effort to conceive what the phenomenon is likely to be at other moments.

For example, a male human creature wakes up in the morning and rises with reluctance. Being a big man, and existing with his wife and children in a very confined space, he has to adapt himself to his environment as he goes through the various functions incident to preparing for his day's work. He is just like you or me. He wants his breakfast, he very much wants to know where his boots are, and he has the usually sinister preoccupations about health and finance. Whatever the force of his egoism, he must more or less harmonise his individuality with those of his wife and children. Having laid down the law, or accepted it, he sets forth to his daily duties, just a fraction of a minute late. He arrives at his office, resumes life with his colleagues sympathetic and antipathetic, and then leaves the office for an expedition extending over several hours. In the course of his expedition he encounters the corpse of a young dog run down by a motor-bus. Now you also have encountered that corpse and are gazing at it; and what do you say to yourself when he comes along? You say: "Oh! Here's a policeman." For he happens to be a policeman. You stare at him, and you never see anything but a policeman—an indivisible phenomenon of blue cloth, steel buttons, flesh resembling a face, and a helmet; "a stalwart guardian of the law"; to you little more human than an algebraic symbol: in a word—a policeman.

Only, that word actually conveys almost nothing to you of the reality which it stands for. You are satisfied with it as you are satisfied with the description of a disease. A friend tells you his eyesight is failing. You sympathise. "What is it?" you ask. "Glaucoma." "Ah! Glaucoma!" You don't know what glaucoma is. You are no wiser than you were before. But you are content. A name has contented you. Similarly the name of policeman contents you, seems to absolve you from further curiosity as to the phenomenon. You have looked at tens of thousands of policemen, and perhaps never seen the hundredth part of the reality of a single one. Your imagination has not truly worked on the phenomenon.

There may be some excuse for not seeing the reality of a policeman, because a uniform is always a thick veil. But you—I mean you, I, any of us—are oddly dim-sighted also in regard to the civil population. For instance, we get into the empty motor-bus as it leaves the scene of the street accident, and examine the men and women who gradually fill it. Probably we vaunt ourselves as being interested in the spectacle of life. All the persons in the motor-bus have come out of a past and are moving towards a future. But how often does our imagination put itself to the trouble of realising this? We may observe with some care, yet owing to a fundamental defect of attitude we are observing not the human individuals, but a peculiar race of beings who pass their whole lives in motor-buses, who exist only in motor-buses and only in the present! No human phenomenon is adequately seen until the imagination has placed it back into its past and forward into its future. And this is the final process of observation of the individual.

* * * * *

23

VII

Seeing life, as I have tried to show, does not begin with seeing the individual. Neither does it end with seeing the individual. Particular and unsystematised observation cannot go on for ever, aimless, formless. Just as individuals are singled out from systems, in the earlier process of observation, so in the later processes individuals will be formed into new groups, which formation will depend upon the personal bent of the observer. The predominant interests of the observer will ultimately direct his observing activities to their own advantage. If he is excited by the phenomena of organisation—as I happen to be—he will see individuals in new groups that are the result of organisation, and will insist on the variations from type due to that grouping. If he is convinced—as numbers of people appear to be—that society is just now in an extremely critical pass, and that if something mysterious is not forthwith done the structure of it will crumble to atoms—he will see mankind grouped under the different reforms which, according to him, the human dilemma demands. And so on! These tendencies, while they should not be resisted too much, since they give character to observation and redeem it from the frigidity of mechanics, should be resisted to a certain extent. For, whatever they may be, they favour the growth of sentimentality, the protean and indescribably subtle enemy of common sense.

* * * * *

PART II.

WRITING NOVELS

I

The novelist is he who, having seen life, and being so excited by it that he absolutely must transmit the vision to others, chooses narrative fiction as the liveliest vehicle for the relief of his feelings. He is like other artists—he cannot remain silent; he cannot keep himself to himself, he is bursting with the news; he is bound to tell—the affair is too thrilling! Only he differs from most artists in this—that what most chiefly strikes him is the indefinable humanness of human nature, the large general manner of existing. Of course, he is the result of evolution from the primitive. And you can see primitive novelists to this day transmitting to acquaintances their fragmentary and crude visions of life in the café or the club, or on the kerbstone. They belong to the lowest circle of artists; but they are artists; and the form that they adopt is the very basis of the novel. By innumerable entertaining steps from them you may ascend to the major artist whose vision of life, inclusive, intricate and intense, requires for its due transmission the great traditional form of the novel as perfected by the masters of a long age which has temporarily set the novel higher than any other art-form.

I would not argue that the novel should be counted supreme among the great traditional forms of art. Even if there is a greatest form, I do

25

not much care which it is. I have in turn been convinced that Chartres Cathedral, certain Greek sculpture, Mozart's *Don Juan*, and the juggling of Paul Cinquevalli, was the finest thing in the world—not to mention the achievements of Shakspere or Nijinsky. But there is something to be said for the real pre-eminence of prose fiction as a literary form. (Even the modern epic has learnt almost all it knows from prose-fiction.) The novel has, and always will have, the advantage of its comprehensive bigness. St Peter's at Rome is a trifle compared with Tolstoi's *War and Peace* ; and it is as certain as anything can be that, during the present geological epoch at any rate, no epic half as long as *War and Peace* will ever be read, even if written.

Notoriously the novelist (including the playwright, who is a sub-novelist) has been taking the bread out of the mouths of other artists. In the matter of poaching, the painter has done a lot, and the composer has done more, but what the painter and the composer have done is as naught compared to the grasping deeds of the novelist. And whereas the painter and the composer have got into difficulties with their audacious schemes, the novelist has poached, colonised, and annexed with a success that is not denied. There is scarcely any aspect of the interestingness of life which is not now rendered in prose fiction—from landscape-painting to sociology—and none which might not be. Unnecessary to go back to the ante-Scott age in order to perceive how the novel has aggrandised itself! It has conquered enormous territories even since *Germinal*. Within the last fifteen years it has gained. Were it to adopt the hue of the British Empire, the entire map of the universe would soon be coloured red. Wherever it ought to stand in the hierarchy of forms, it has, actually, no rival at the present day as a means for transmitting the impassioned vision of life. It is, and will be for some time to come, the form to which the artist with the most inclusive vision instinctively turns, because it is the most inclusive form, and the most adaptable. Indeed, before we are much older, if its present rate of progress continues, it will have reoccupied the dazzling position to which the mighty Balzac lifted it, and in which he left it in 1850. So much, by the way, for the rank of the novel.

* * * * *

II

In considering the equipment of the novelist there are two attributes which may always be taken for granted. The first is the sense of beauty—indispensable to the creative artist. Every creative artist has it, in his degree. He is an artist because he has it. An artist works under the stress of instinct. No man's instinct can draw him towards material which repels him—the fact is obvious. Obviously, whatever kind of life the novelist writes about, he has been charmed and seduced by it, he is under its spell—that is, he has seen beauty in it. He could have no other reason for writing about it. He may see a strange sort of beauty; he may—indeed he does—see a sort of beauty that nobody has quite seen before; he may see a sort of beauty that none save a few odd spirits ever will or can be made to see. But he does see beauty. To say, after reading a novel which has held you, that the author has no sense of beauty, is inept. (The mere fact that you turned over his pages with interest is an answer to the criticism—a criticism, indeed, which is not more sagacious than that of the reviewer who remarks: "Mr Blank has produced a thrilling novel, but unfortunately he cannot write." Mr Blank has written; and he could, anyhow, write enough to thrill the reviewer.) All that a wise person will assert is that an artist's sense of beauty is different for the time being from his own.

The reproach of the lack of a sense of beauty has been brought against nearly all original novelists; it is seldom brought against a mediocre novelist. Even in the extreme cases it is untrue; perhaps it is most untrue in the extreme cases. I do not mean such a case as that of Zola, who never went to extremes. I mean, for example, Gissing, a real extremist, who, it is now admitted, saw a clear and undiscovered beauty in forms of existence which hitherto no artist had deigned seriously to examine. And I mean Huysmans, a case even more extreme. Possibly no works have been more abused for ugliness than Huysman's novel *En Ménage* and his book of descriptive essays *De Tout*. Both reproduce with exasperation what is generally regarded as the sordid ugliness of commonplace daily life. Yet both exercise a unique charm (and will surely be read when *La Cathédrale* is forgotten). And it is inconceivable that Huysmans—whatever he may have said—was not ravished by the secret beauty of his subjects and did not exult in it.

The other attribute which may be taken for granted in the novelist, as in every artist, is passionate intensity of vision. Unless the vision is passionately intense the artist will not be moved to transmit it. He will not be inconvenienced by it; and the motive to pass it on will thus not exist. Every fine emotion produced in the reader has been, and must have been, previously felt by the writer, but in a far greater degree. It is not altogether uncommon to hear a reader whose heart has been desolated by the poignancy of a narrative complain that the writer is unemotional. Such people have no notion at all of the processes of artistic creation.

* * * * *

III

A sense of beauty and a passionate intensity of vision being taken for granted, the one other important attribute in the equipment of the novelist—the attribute which indeed by itself practically suffices, and whose absence renders futile all the rest—is fineness of mind. A great novelist must have great qualities of mind. His mind must be sympathetic, quickly responsive, courageous, honest, humorous, tender, just, merciful.

He must be able to conceive the ideal without losing sight of the fact that it is a human world we live in. Above all, his mind must be permeated and controlled by common sense. His mind, in a word, must have the quality of being noble. Unless his mind is all this, he will never, at the ultimate bar, be reckoned supreme. That which counts, on every page, and all the time, is the very texture of his mind—the glass through which he sees things. Every other attribute is secondary, and is dispensable. Fielding lives unequalled among English novelists because the broad nobility of his mind is unequalled. He is read with unreserved enthusiasm because the reader feels himself at each paragraph to be in close contact with a glorious personality. And no advance in technique among later novelists can possibly imperil his position. He will take second place when a more noble mind, a more superb common sense, happens to wield the narrative pen, and not before. What undermines the renown of Dickens is the growing conviction that the texture of his mind was common, that he fell short in courageous facing of the truth, and in certain delicacies of perception. As much may be said of Thackeray, whose mind was somewhat incomplete for so grandiose a figure, and not free from defects which are inimical to immortality.

It is a hard saying for me, and full of danger in any country whose artists have shown contempt for form, yet I am obliged to say that, as the years pass, I attach less and less importance to good technique in fiction. I love it, and I have fought for a better recognition of its importance in England, but I now have to admit that the modern history of fiction will not support me. With the single exception of Turgenev, the great novelists of the world, according to my own standards, have either ignored technique or have failed to understand it. What an error to suppose that the finest foreign novels show a better sense of form than the finest English novels! Balzac was a prodigious blunderer. He could not even manage a sentence, not to speak of the general form of a book. And as for a greater than Balzac—Stendhal—his scorn of technique was notorious. Stendhal was capable of writing, in a masterpiece: "By the way

I ought to have told you earlier that the Duchess——!" And as for a greater than either Balzac or Stendhal—Dostoievsky—what a hasty, amorphous lump of gold is the sublime, the unapproachable *Brothers Karamazov*! Any tutor in a college for teaching the whole art of fiction by post in twelve lessons could show where Dostoievsky was clumsy and careless. What would have been Flaubert's detailed criticism of that book? And what would it matter? And, to take a minor example, witness the comically amateurish technique of the late "Mark Rutherford"—nevertheless a novelist whom one can deeply admire.

And when we come to consider the great technicians, Guy de Maupassant and Flaubert, can we say that their technique will save them, or atone in the slightest degree for the defects of their minds? Exceptional artists both, they are both now inevitably falling in esteem to the level of the second-rate. Human nature being what it is, and de Maupassant being tinged with eroticism, his work is sure to be read with interest by mankind; but he is already classed. Nobody, now, despite all his brilliant excellences, would dream of putting de Maupassant with the first magnitudes. And the declension of Flaubert is one of the outstanding phenomena of modern French criticism. It is being discovered that Flaubert's mind was not quite noble enough—that, indeed, it was a cruel mind, and a little anæmic. *Bouvard et Pécuchet* was the crowning proof that Flaubert had lost sight of the humanness of the world, and suffered from the delusion that he had been born on the wrong planet. The glitter of his technique is dulled now, and fools even count it against him. In regard to one section of human activity only did his mind seem noble—namely, literary technique. His correspondence, written, of course, currently, was largely occupied with the question of literary technique, and his correspondence stands forth to-day as his best work—a marvellous fount of inspiration to his fellow artists. So I return to the point that the novelist's one important attribute (beyond the two postulated) is fundamental quality of mind. It and nothing else makes both the friends and the enemies which he has;

while the influence of technique is slight and transitory. And I repeat that it is a hard saying.

I begin to think that great writers of fiction are by the mysterious nature of their art ordained to be "amateurs." There may be something of the amateur in all great artists. I do not know why it should be so, unless because, in the exuberance of their sense of power, they are impatient of the exactitudes of systematic study and the mere bother of repeated attempts to arrive at a minor perfection. Assuredly no great artist was ever a profound scholar. The great artist has other ends to achieve. And every artist, major and minor, is aware in his conscience that art is full of artifice, and that the desire to proceed rapidly with the affair of creation, and an excus able dislike of re-creating anything twice, thrice, or ten times over—unnatural task!—are responsible for much of that artifice. We can all point in excuse to Shakspere, who was a very rough-and-ready person, and whose methods would shock Flaubert. Indeed, the amateurishness of Shakspere has been mightily exposed of late years. But nobody seems to care. If Flaubert had been a greater artist he might have been more of an amateur.

* * * * *

IV

Of this poor neglected matter of technique the more important branch is design—or construction. It is the branch of the art—of all arts—which comes next after "inspiration"—a capacious word meant to include everything that the artist must be born with and cannot acquire. The less important branch of technique—far less important—may be described as an ornamentation.

There are very few rules of design in the novel; but the few are capital. Nevertheless, great novelists have often flouted or ignored them—to the detriment of their work. In my opinion the first rule is that the interest must be centralised; it must not be diffused equally over various parts of the canvas. To compare one art with another may be perilous, but really the convenience of describing a novel as a canvas is extreme. In a well-designed picture the eye is drawn chiefly to one particular spot. If the eye is drawn with equal force to several different spots, then we reproach the painter for having "scattered" the interest of the picture. Similarly with the novel. A novel must have one, two, or three figures that easily overtop the rest. These figures must be in the foreground, and the rest in the middle-distance or in the back-ground.

Moreover, these figures—whether they are saints or sinners—must somehow be presented more sympathetically than the others. If this cannot be done, then the inspiration is at fault. The single motive that should govern the choice of a principal figure is the motive of love for that figure. What else could the motive be? The race of heroes is essential to art. But what makes a hero is less the deeds of the figure chosen than the understanding sympathy of the artist with the figure. To say that the hero has disappeared from modern fiction is absurd. All that has happened is that the characteristics of the hero have changed, naturally, with the times. When Thackeray wrote "a novel without a hero," he wrote a novel with a first-class hero, and nobody knew this better than Thackeray. What he meant was that he was sick of the conventional bundle of characteristics styled a hero in his day, and that he had changed the type. Since then we have grown sick of Dobbins, and the type has been changed again more than once. The fateful hour will arrive when we shall be sick of Ponderevos.

The temptation of the great novelist, overflowing with creative force, is to scatter the interest. In both his major works Tolstoi found the temptation too strong for him. *Anna Karenina* is not one novel, but two, and suffers accordingly. As for *War and Peace*, the reader wanders about in it as in a forest, for days, lost, deprived of a sense of direction, and with no vestige of a sign-post; at intervals encountering mysterious faces whose identity he in vain tries to recall. On a much smaller scale Meredith committed the same error. Who could assert positively which of the sisters Fleming is the heroine of *Rhoda Fleming* ? For nearly two hundred pages at a stretch Rhoda scarcely appears. And more than once the author seems quite to forget that the little knave Algernon is not, after all, the hero of the story.

The second rule of design—perhaps in the main merely a different view of the first—is that the interest must be maintained. It may increase, but it must never diminish. Here is that special aspect of design which we call construction, or plot. By interest I mean the interest of the story itself, and not the interest of the continual play of the author's mind on his material. In proportion as the interest of the story is maintained, the plot is a good one. In so far as it lapses, the plot is a bad one. There is no other criterion of good con struction. Readers of a certain class are apt to call good the plot of that story in which "you can't tell what is going to happen next." But in some of the most tedious novels ever written you can't tell what is going to happen next—and you don't care a fig what is going to happen next. It would be nearer the mark to say that the plot is good when "you want to make sure what will happen next"! Good plots set you anxiously guessing what will happen next.

When the reader is misled—not intentionally in order to get an effect, but clumsily through amateurishness—then the construction is bad. This calamity does not often occur in fine novels, but in really good work another calamity does occur with far too much frequency—namely, the tantalising of the reader at a critical point by a purposeless, wanton, or negligent shifting of the interest from the major to the minor theme. A sad example of this infantile trick is to be found in the thirty-first chapter of *Rhoda Fleming*, wherein, well knowing that the reader is tingling for the interview between Roberts and Rhoda, the author, unable to control his own capricious and monstrous fancy for Algernon, devotes some sixteen pages to the young knave's vagaries with an illicit thousand pounds. That the sixteen pages are excessively brilliant does not a bit excuse the wilful unshapeliness of the book's design.

The Edwardian and Georgian out-and-out defenders of Victorian fiction are wont to argue that though the event-plot in sundry great novels may be loose and casual (that is to say, simply careless), the "idea-plot" is usually close-knit, coherent, and logical. I have never yet been able to comprehend how an idea-plot can exist independently of an event-plot (any more than how spirit can be conceived apart from matter); but assuming that an idea-plot can exist independently, and that the mysterious thing is superior in form to its coarse fellow, the event-plot (which I positively do not believe),—even then I still hold that sloppiness in the fabrication of the event-plot amounts to a grave iniquity. In this connection I have in mind, among English novels, chiefly the work of "Mark Rutherford," George Eliot, the Brontës, and Anthony Trollope.

The one other important rule in construction is that the plot should be kept throughout within the same convention. All plots—even those of our most sacred naturalistic contemporaries—are and must be a conventionalisation of life. We imagine we have arrived at a convention which is nearer to the truth of life than that of our forerunners. Perhaps we have—but so little nearer that the difference is scarcely appreciable! An aviator at midday may be nearer the sun than the motorist, but regarded as a portion of the entire journey to the sun, the aviator's progress upward can safely be ignored. No novelist has yet, or ever will, come within a hundred million miles of life itself. It is impossible for us to see how far we still are from life. The defects of a new convention disclose themselves late in its career. The notion that "naturalists" have at last lighted on a final formula which ensures truth to life is ridiculous. "Naturalist" is merely an epithet expressing self-satisfaction.

Similarly, the habit of deriding as "conventional" plots constructed in an earlier convention, is ridiculous. Under this head Dickens in particular has been assaulted; I have assaulted him myself. But within their convention, the plots of Dickens are excellent, and show little trace of amateurishness, and every sign of skilled accomplishment. And Dickens did not blunder out of one convention into another, as certain of ourselves undeniably do. Thomas Hardy, too, has been arraigned for the conventionalism of his plots. And yet Hardy happens to be one of the rare novelists who have evolved a new convention to suit their idiosyncrasy. Hardy's idiosyncrasy is a deep conviction of the whimsicality of the divine power, and again and again he has expressed this with a virtuosity of skill which ought to have put humility into the hearts of naturalists, but which has not done so. The plot of *The Woodlanders* is one of the most exquisite examples of subtle symbolic illustration of an idea that a writer of fiction ever achieved; it makes the symbolism of Ibsen seem crude. You may say that *The Woodlanders* could not have occurred in real life. No novel could have occurred in real life. The balance of probabilities is incalculably against any novel whatsoever; and rightly so. A convention is essential, and the duty of a novelist is to be true within his chosen convention, and not further. Most novelists still fail in this duty. Is there any reason, indeed, why we should be so vastly cleverer than our fathers? I do not think we are.

* * * * *

V

Leaving the seductive minor question of ornamentation, I come lastly to the question of getting the semblance of life on to the page before the eyes of the reader—the daily and hourly texture of existence. The novelist has selected his subject; he has drenched himself in his subject. He has laid down the main features of the design. The living embryo is there, and waits to be developed into full organic structure. Whence and how does the novelist obtain the vital tissue which must be his material? The answer is that he digs it out of himself. First-class fiction is, and must be, in the final resort autobiographical. What else should it be? The novelist may take notes of phenomena likely to be of use to him. And he may acquire the skill to invent very apposite illustrative inci dent. But he cannot invent psychology. Upon occasion some human being may entrust him with confidences extremely precious for his craft. But such windfalls are so rare as to be negligible. From outward symptoms he can guess something of the psychology of others. He can use a real person as the unrecognisable but helpful basis for each of his characters . . . And all that is nothing. And all special research is nothing. When the real intimate work of creation has to be done—and it has to be done on every page—the novelist can only look within for effective aid. Almost solely by arranging and modifying what he has felt and seen, and scarcely at all by inventing, can he accomplish his end. An inquiry into the career of any first-class novelist invariably reveals that his novels are full of autobiography. But, as a fact, every good novel contains far more autobiography than any inquiry could reveal. Episodes, moods, characters of autobiography can be detected and traced to their origin by critical acumen, but the intimate autobiography that runs through each page, vitalising it, may not be detected. In dealing with each character in each episode the novelist must for a thousand convincing details interrogate that part of his own individuality which corresponds to the particular character. The foundation of his equipment is universal sympathy. And the result of this (or the cause—I don't know which) is that in his own individuality there is something of everybody. If he is a born novelist he is safe in asking himself, when in doubt as to the behaviour of a given personage at a given point: "Now, what should *I* have done?" And incorporating the answer! And this in practice is what he does. Good fiction is autobiography dressed in the colours of all mankind.

The necessarily autobiographical nature of fiction accounts for the creative repetition to which all novelists—including the most powerful—are reduced. They monotonously yield again and again to the strongest predilections of their own individuality. Again and again they think they are creating, by observation, a quite new character—and lo! when finished it is an old one—autobiographical psychology has triumphed! A novelist may achieve a reputation with only a single type, created and re-created in varying forms. And the very greatest do not contrive to create more than half a score genuine separate types. In Cerfberr and Christophe's biographical dictionary of the characters of Balzac, a tall volume of six hundred pages, there are some two thousand entries of different individuals, but probably fewer than a dozen genuine distinctive types. No creative artist ever repeated himself more brazenly or more successfully than Balzac. His miser, his vicious delightful actress, his vicious delightful duchess, his young man-about-town, his virtuous young man, his heroic weeping virgin, his angelic wife and mother, his poor relation, and his faithful stupid servant—each is continually popping up with a new name in the Human Comedy. A similar phenomenon, as Frank Harris has proved, is to be observed in Shakspere. Hamlet of Denmark was only the last and greatest of a series of Shaksperean Hamlets.

It may be asked, finally: What of the actual process of handling the raw material dug out of existence and of the artist's self—the process of transmuting life into art? There is no process. That is to say, there is no conscious process. The convention chosen by an artist is his illusion of the truth. Consciously, the artist only omits, selects, arranges. But let him beware of being false to his illusion, for then the process becomes conscious, and bad. This is sentimentality, which is the seed of death in his work. Every artist is tempted to sentimentalise, or to be cynical—practically the same thing. And when he falls to the temptation, the reader whispers in his heart, be it only for one instant: "That is not true to life." And in turn the reader's illusion of reality is impaired. Readers are divided into two classes—the enemies and the friends of the artist. The former, a legion, admire for a fortnight or a year. They hate an uncompromising struggle for the truth. They positively like the artist to fall to temptation. If he falls, they exclaim, "How sweet!" The latter are capable of savouring the fine unpleasantness of the struggle for truth.

And when they whisper in their hearts: "That is not true to life," they are ashamed for the artist. They are few, very few; but a vigorous clan. It is they who confer immortality.

* * * * *

PART III.

WRITING PLAYS

I

There is an idea abroad, assiduously fostered as a rule by critics who happen to have written neither novels nor plays, that it is more difficult to write a play than a novel. I do not think so. I have written or collaborated in about twenty novels and about twenty plays, and I am convinced that it is easier to write a play than a novel. Personally, I would sooner *write* two plays than one novel; less expenditure of nervous force and mere brains would be required for two plays than for one novel. (I emphasise the word "write," because if the whole weariness between the first conception and the first performance of a play is compared with the whole weariness between the first conception and the first publication of a novel, then the play has it. I would sooner get seventy-and-seven novels produced than one play. But my immediate object is to compare only writing with writing.) It seems to me that the sole persons entitled to judge of the comparative difficulty of writing plays and writing novels are those authors who have succeeded or failed equally well in both departments. And in this limited band I imagine that the differences of opinion on the point could not be marked. I would like to note in passing, for the support of my proposition, that whereas established novelists not infrequently venture into the theatre with audacity, established dramatists are very cautious indeed about quitting the theatre. An established dramatist usually takes good care to write plays and naught else; he will not affront the risks of coming out into the open; and therein his instinct is quite properly that of self-preservation. Of many established dramatists all over the world it may be affirmed that if they were so indiscreet as to publish a novel, the result would be a great shattering and a great awakening.

* * * * *

II

An enormous amount of vague reverential nonsense is talked about the technique of the stage, the assumption being that in difficulty it far surpasses any other literary technique, and that until it is acquired a respectable play cannot be written. One hears also that it can only be acquired behind the scenes. A famous actor-manager once kindly gave me the benefit of his experience, and what he said was that a dramatist who wished to learn his business must live behind the scenes—and study the works of Dion Boucicault! The truth is that no technique is so crude and so simple as the technique of the stage, and that the proper place to learn it is not behind the scenes but in the pit. Managers, being the most conservative people on earth, except compositors, will honestly try to convince the naïve dramatist that effects can only be obtained in the precise way in which effects have always been obtained, and that this and that rule must not be broken on pain of outraging the public.

And indeed it is natural that managers should talk thus, seeing the low state of the drama, because in any art rules and reaction always flourish when creative energy is sick. The mandarins have ever said and will ever say that a technique which does not correspond with their own is no technique, but simple clumsiness. There are some seven situations in the customary drama, and a play which does not contain at least one of those situations in each act will be condemned as "undramatic," or "thin," or as being "all talk." It may contain half a hundred other situations, but for the mandarin a situation which is not one of the seven is not a situation. Similarly there are some dozen character types in the customary drama, and all original that is, truthful—characterisation will be dismissed as a total absence of characterisation because it does not reproduce any of these dozen types. Thus every truly original play is bound to be indicted for bad technique. The author is bound to be told that what he has written may be marvellously clever, but that it is not a play. I remember the day—and it is not long ago—when even so experienced and sincere a critic as William Archer used to argue that if the "intellectual" drama did not succeed with the general public, it was because its technique was not up to the level of the technique of the commercial drama! Perhaps he has changed his opinion since then. Heaven knows that the so-called "intellectual" drama is amateurish enough, but nearly all literary art is amateurish, and assuredly no intellectual drama could hope to compete in clumsiness with some of the most successful commercial plays of modern times. I tremble to think what the mandarins and William Archer would say to the technique of *Hamlet*, could it by some miracle be brought forward as a new piece by a Mr Shakspere. They would probably recommend Mr Shakspere to consider the ways of Sardou, Henri Bernstein, and Sir Herbert Tree, and be wise. Most positively they would assert that *Hamlet* was not a play. And their pupils of the daily press would point out— what surely Mr Shakspere ought to have perceived for himself—that the second, third, or fourth act might be cut wholesale without the slightest loss to the piece.

In the sense in which mandarins understand the word technique, there is no technique special to the stage except that which concerns the moving of solid human bodies to and fro, and the limitations of the human senses. The dramatist must not expect his audience to be able to see or hear two things at once, nor to be incapable of fatigue. And he must not expect his interpreters to stroll round or come on or go off in a satisfactory manner unless he provides them with satisfactory reasons for strolling round, coming on, or going off. Lastly, he must not expect his interpreters to achieve physical impossibilities. The dramatist who sends a pretty woman off in street attire and seeks to bring her on again in thirty seconds fully dressed for a court ball may fail in stage technique, but he has not proved that stage technique is tremendously difficult; he has proved something quite else.

* * * * *

III

One reason why a play is easier to write than a novel is that a play is shorter than a novel. On the average, one may say that it takes six plays to make the matter of a novel. Other things being equal, a short work of art presents fewer difficulties than a longer one. The contrary is held true by the majority, but then the majority, having never attempted to produce a long work of art, are unqualified to offer an opinion. It is said that the most difficult form of poetry is the sonnet. But the most difficult form of poetry is the epic. The proof that the sonnet is the most difficult form is alleged to be in the fewness of perfect sonnets. There are, however, far more perfect sonnets than perfect epics. A perfect sonnet may be a heavenly accident. But such accidents can never happen to writers of epics. Some years ago we had an enormous palaver about the "art of the short story," which numerous persons who had omitted to write novels pronounced to be more difficult than the novel. But the fact remains that there are scores of perfect short stories, whereas it is doubtful whether anybody but Turgenev ever did write a perfect novel. A short form is easier to manipulate than a long form, because its construction is less complicated, because the balance of its proportions can be more easily corrected by means of a rapid survey, because it is lawful and even necessary in it to leave undone many things which are very hard to do, and because the emotional strain is less prolonged. The most difficult thing in all art is to maintain the imaginative tension unslackened throughout a considerable period.

Then, not only does a play contain less matter than a novel—it is further simplified by the fact that it contains fewer kinds of matter, and less subtle kinds of matter. There are numerous delicate and difficult affairs of craft that the dramatist need not think about at all. If he attempts to go beyond a certain very mild degree of subtlety, he is merely wasting his time. What passes for subtle on the stage would have a very obvious air in a novel, as some dramatists have unhappily discovered. Thus whole continents of danger may be shunned by the dramatist, and instead of being scorned for his cowardice he will be very rightly applauded for his artistic discretion. Fortunate predicament! Again, he need not—indeed, he must not—save in a primitive and hinting manner, concern himself with "atmosphere." He may roughly suggest one, but if he begins on the feat of "creating" an atmosphere (as it is called), the last suburban train will have departed before he has reached the crisis of the play. The last suburban train is the best friend of the dramatist, though the fellow seldom has the sense to see it. Further, he is saved all de scriptive work. See a novelist harassing himself into his grave over the description of a landscape, a room, a gesture—while the dramatist grins. The dramatist may have to imagine a landscape, a room, or a gesture; but he has not got to write it—and it is the writing which hastens death. If a dramatist and a novelist set out to portray a clever woman, they are almost equally matched, because each has to make the creature say things and do things. But if they set out to portray a charming woman, the dramatist can recline in an easy chair and smoke while the novelist is ruining temper, digestion and eyesight, and spreading terror in his household by his moodiness and unapproachability. The electric light burns in the novelist's study at three a.m.,—the novelist is still endeavouring to convey by means of words the extraordinary fascination that his heroine could exercise over mankind by

43

the mere act of walking into a room; and he never has really succeeded and never will. The dramatist writes curtly, "Enter Millicent." All are anxious to do the dramatist's job for him. Is the play being read at home—the reader eagerly and with brilliant success puts his imagination to work and completes a charming Millicent after his own secret desires. (Whereas he would coldly decline to add one touch to Millicent were she the heroine of a novel.) Is the play being performed on the stage—an experienced, conscientious, and perhaps lovely actress will strive her hardest to prove that the dramatist was right about Millicent's astounding fascination. And if she fails, nobody will blame the dramatist; the dramatist will receive naught but sympathy.

And there is still another region of superlative difficulty which is narrowly circumscribed for the spoilt dramatist: I mean the whole business of persuading the public that the improbable is probable. Every work of art is and must be crammed with improbabilities and artifice; and the greater portion of the artifice is employed in just this trickery of persuasion. Only, the public of the dramatist needs far less persuading than the public of the novelist. The novelist announces that Millicent accepted the hand of the wrong man, and in spite of all the novelist's corroborative and exegetical detail the insulted reader declines to credit the statement and condemns the incident as unconvincing. The dramatist decides that Millicent must accept the hand of the wrong man, and there she is on the stage in flesh and blood, veritably doing it! Not easy for even the critical beholder to maintain that Millicent could not and did not do such a silly thing when he has actually with his eyes seen her in the very act! The dramatist, as usual, having done less, is more richly rewarded by results.

Of course it will be argued, as it has always been argued, by those who have not written novels, that it is precisely the "doing less"—the leaving out—that constitutes the unique and fearful difficulty of dramatic art. "The skill to leave out"—lo! the master faculty of the dramatist! But, in the first place, I do not believe that, having regard to the relative scope of the play and of the novel, the necessity for leaving out is more acute in the one than in the other. The adjective "photographic" is as absurd applied to the novel as to the play. And, in the second place, other factors being equal, it is less exhausting, and it requires less skill, to refrain from doing than to do. To know when to refrain from doing may be hard, but positively to do is even harder. Sometimes, listening to partisans of the drama, I have been moved to suggest that, if the art of omission is so wondrously difficult, a dramatist who practised the habit of omitting to write anything whatever ought to be hailed as the supreme craftsman.

* * * * *

IV

The more closely one examines the subject, the more clear and certain becomes the fact that there is only one fundamental artistic difference between the novel and the play, and that difference (to which I shall come later) is not the difference which would be generally named as distinguishing the play from the novel. The apparent differences are superficial, and are due chiefly to considerations of convenience.

Whether in a play or in a novel the creative artist has to tell a story—using the word story in a very wide sense. Just as a novel is divided into chapters, and for a similar reason, a play is divided into acts. But neither chapters nor acts are necessary. Some of Balzac's chief novels have no chapter-divisions, and it has been proved that a theatre audience can and will listen for two hours to "talk," and even recitative singing, on the stage, without a pause. Indeed, audiences, under the compulsion of an artist strong and imperious enough, could, I am sure, be trained to marvellous feats of prolonged receptivity. However, chapters and acts are usual, and they involve the same constructional processes on the part of the artist. The entire play or novel must tell a complete story—that is, arouse a curiosity and reasonably satisfy it, raise a main question and then settle it. And each act or other chief division must tell a definite portion of the story, satisfy part of the curiosity, settle part of the question. And each scene or other minor division must do the same according to its scale. Everything basic that applies to the technique of the novel applies equally to the technique of the play.

In particular, I would urge that a play, any more than a novel, need not be dramatic, employing the term as it is usually employed. In so far as it suspends the listener's interest, every tale, however told, may be said to be dramatic. In this sense *The Golden Bowl* is dramatic; so are *Dominique* and *Persuasion*. A play need not be more dramatic than that. Very emphatically a play need not be dramatic in the stage sense. It need never induce interest to the degree of excitement. It need have nothing that resembles what would be recognisable in the theatre as a situation. It may amble on—and it will still be a play, and it may succeed in pleasing either the fastidious hundreds or the unfastidious hundreds of thousands, according to the talent of the author. Without doubt mandarins will continue for about a century yet to excommunicate certain plays from the category of plays. But nobody will be any the worse. And dramatists will go on proving that whatever else divides a play from a book, "dramatic quality" does not. Some arch-Mandarin may launch at me one of those mandarinic epigram matic questions which are supposed to overthrow the adversary at one dart. "Do you seriously mean to argue, sir, that drama need not be dramatic?" I do, if the word dramatic is to be used in the mandarinic signification. I mean to state that some of the finest plays of the modern age differ from a psychological novel in nothing but the superficial form of telling. Example, Henri Becque's *La Parisienne*, than which there is no better. If I am asked to give my own definition of the adjective "dramatic," I would say that that story is dramatic which is told in dialogue imagined to be spoken by actors and actresses on the stage, and that any narrower definition is bound to exclude some genuine plays universally accepted as such—even by mandarins. For be it noted that the mandarin is never consistent.

My definition brings me to the sole technical difference between a play and a novel—in the play the story is told by means of a dialogue. It is a difference less important than it seems, and not invariably even a sure point of distinction between the two kinds of narrative. For a novel may consist exclusively of dialogue. And plays may contain other matter than dialogue. The classic chorus is not dialogue. But nowadays we should consider the device of the chorus to be clumsy, as, nowadays, it indeed would be. We have grown very ingenious and clever at the trickery of making characters talk to the audience and explain themselves and their past history while seemingly innocent of any such intention. And here, I admit, the dramatist has to face a difficulty special to himself, which the novelist can avoid. I believe it to be the sole difficulty which is peculiar to the drama, and that it is not acute is proved by the ease with which third-rate dramatists have generally vanquished it. Mandarins are wont to assert that the dramatist is also handicapped by the necessity for rigid economy in the use of material. This is not so. Rigid economy in the use of material is equally advisable in every form of art. If it is a necessity, it is a necessity which all artists flout from time to time, and occasionally with gorgeous results, and the successful dramatist has hitherto not been less guilty of flouting it than the novelist or any other artist.

* * * * *

V

And now, having shown that some alleged differences between the play and the novel are illusory, and that a certain technical difference, though possibly real, is superficial and slight, I come to the fundamental difference between them—a difference which the laity does not suspect, which is seldom insisted upon and never sufficiently, but which nobody who is well versed in the making of both plays and novels can fail to feel profoundly. The emotional strain of writing a play is not merely less prolonged than that of writing a novel, it is less severe even while it lasts, lower in degree and of a less purely creative character. And herein is the chief of all the reasons why a play is easier to write than a novel. The drama does not belong exclusively to literature, because its effect depends on something more than the composition of words. The dramatist is the sole author of a play, but he is not the sole creator of it. Without him nothing can be done, but, on the other hand, he cannot do everything himself. He begins the work of creation, which is finished either by creative interpreters on the stage, or by the creative imagination of the reader in the study. It is as if he carried an immense weight to the landing at the turn of a flight of stairs, and that thence upward the lifting had to be done by other people. Consider the affair as a pyramidal structure, and the dramatist is the base—but he is not the apex. A play is a collaboration of creative faculties. The egotism of the dramatist resents this uncomfortable fact, but the fact exists. And further, the creative faculties are not only those of the author, the stage-director ("producer") and the actors—the audience itself is unconsciously part of the collaboration.

Hence a dramatist who attempts to do the whole work of creation before the acting begins is an inartistic usurper of the functions of others, and will fail of proper accomplishment at the end. The dramatist must deliberately, in performing his share of the work, leave scope for a multitude of alien faculties whose operations he can neither precisely foresee nor completely control. The point is not that in the writing of a play there are various sorts of matters—as we have already seen—which the dramatist must ignore; the point is that even in the region proper to him he must not push the creative act to its final limit. He must ever remember those who are to come after him. For instance, though he must visualise a scene as he writes it, he should not visualise it completely, as a novelist should. The novelist may perceive vividly the faces of his personages, but if the playwright insists on seeing faces, either he will see the faces of real actors and hamper himself by moulding the scene to suit such real actors, or he will perceive imaginary faces, and the ultimate interpretation will perforce falsify his work and nullify his intentions. This aspect of the subject might well be much amplified, but only for a public of practising dramatists.

* * * * *

VI

When the play is "finished," the processes of collaboration have yet to begin. The serious work of the dramatist is over, but the most desolating part of his toil awaits him. I do not refer to the business of arranging with a theatrical manager for the production of the play. For, though that generally partakes of the nature of tragedy, it also partakes of the nature of amusing burlesque, owing to the fact that theatrical managers are—no doubt inevitably—theatrical. Nevertheless, even the theatrical manager, while disclaiming the slightest interest in anything more vital to the stage than the box-office, is himself in some degree a collaborator, and is the first to show to the dramatist that a play is not a play till it is performed. The manager reads the play, and, to the dramatist's astonishment, reads quite a different play from that which the dramatist imagines he wrote. In particular the manager reads a play which can scarcely hope to succeed—indeed, a play against whose chances of success ten thousand powerful reasons can be adduced. It is remarkable that a manager nearly always foresees failure in a manuscript, and very seldom success. The manager's profoundest instinct—self-preservation again!—is to refuse a play; if he accepts, it is against the grain, against his judgment—and out of a mad spirit of adventure. Some of the most glittering successes have been rehearsed in an atmosphere of settled despair. The dramatist naturally feels an immense contempt for the opinions artistic and otherwise of the manager, and he is therein justified. The manager's vocation is not to write plays, nor (let us hope) to act in them, nor to direct the rehearsals of them, and even his knowledge of the vagaries of his own box-office has often proved to be pitiably delusive. The manager's true and only vocation is to refrain from producing plays. Despite all this, however, the manager has already collaborated in the play. The dramatist sees it differently now. All sorts of new considerations have been presented to him. Not a word has been altered; but it is noticeably another play. Which is merely to say that the creative work on it which still remains to be done has been more accurately envisaged. This strange experience could not happen to a novel, because when a novel is written it is finished.

And when the director of rehearsals, or producer, has been chosen, and this priceless and mysterious person has his first serious confabulation with the author, then at once the play begins to assume new shapes— contours undreamt of by the author till that startling moment. And even if the author has the temerity to conduct his own rehearsals, similar disconcerting phenomena will occur; for the author as a producer is a different fellow from the author as author. The producer is up against realities. He, first, renders the play concrete, gradually condenses its filmy vapours into a solid element . . . He suggests the casting. "What do you think of X. for the old man?" asks the producer. The author is staggered. Is it conceivable that so renowned a producer can have so misread and misunderstood the play? X. would be preposterous as the old man. But the producer goes on talking. And suddenly the author sees possibilities in X. But at the same time he sees a different play from what he wrote. And quite probably he sees a more glorious play. Quite probably he had not suspected how great a dramatist he is . . . Before the first rehearsal is called, the play, still without a word altered, has gone through astounding creative transmutations; the author recognises in it some likeness to his beloved child, but it is the likeness of a first cousin.

At the first rehearsal, and for many rehearsals, to an extent perhaps increasing, perhaps decreasing, the dramatist is forced into an apologetic and self-conscious mood; and his mien is something between that of a criminal who has committed a horrid offence and that of a father over the crude body of a new-born child. Now in truth he deeply realises that the play is a collaboration. In extreme cases he may be brought to see that he himself is one of the less important factors in the collaboration. The first preoccupation of the interpreters is not with his play at all, but—quite rightly—with their own careers; if they were not honestly convinced that their own careers were the chief genuine excuse for the existence of the theatre and the play they would not act very well. But, more than that, they do not regard his play as a sufficient vehicle for the furtherance of their careers. At the most favourable, what they secretly think is that if they are permitted to exercise their talents on his play there is a chance that they may be able to turn it into a sufficient vehicle for the furtherance of their careers. The attitude of every actor towards his part is: "My part is not much of a part as it stands, but if my individuality is allowed to get into free contact with it, I may make something brilliant out of it." Which attitude is a proper attitude, and an attitude in my opinion justified by the facts of the case. The actor's phrase is that he *creates* a part, and he is right. He completes the labour of creation begun by the author and continued by the producer, and if reasonable liberty is not accorded to him—if either the author or the producer attempts to do too much of the creative work—the result cannot be satisfactory.

As the rehearsals proceed the play changes from day to day. However autocratic the producer, however obstinate the dramatist, the play will vary at each rehearsal like a large cloud in a gentle wind. It is never the same play for two days together. Nor is this surprising, seeing that every day and night a dozen, or it may be two dozen, human beings endowed with the creative gift are creatively working on it. Every dramatist who is candid with himself—I do not suggest that he should be candid to the theatrical world—well knows that though his play is often worsened by his collaborators it is also often improved,—and improved in the most mysterious and dazzling manner—without a word being altered. Producer and actors do not merely suggest possibilities, they execute them. And the author is confronted by artistic phenomena for which lawfully he may not claim credit. On the other hand, he may be confronted by inartistic phenomena in respect to which lawfully he is blameless, but which he cannot prevent; a rehearsal is like a battle,—certain persons are theoretically in control, but in fact the thing principally fights itself. And thus the creation goes on until the dress-rehearsal, when it seems to have come to a stop. And the dramatist lying awake in the night reflects, stoically, fatalistically: "Well, that is the play that they have made of *my* play!" And he may be pleased or he may be disgusted. But if he attends the first performance he cannot fail to notice, after the first few minutes of it, that he was quite mistaken, and that what the actors are performing is still another play. The audience is collaborating.

* * * * *

PART IV.

THE ARTIST AND THE PUBLIC

I

I can divide all the imaginative writers I have ever met into two classes—those who admitted and sometimes proclaimed loudly that they desired popularity; and those who expressed a noble scorn or a gentle contempt for popularity. The latter, however, always failed to conceal their envy of popular authors, and this envy was a phenomenon whose truculent bitterness could not be surpassed even in political or religious life. And indeed, since (as I have held in a previous chapter) the object of the artist is to share his emotions with others, it would be strange if the normal artist spurned popularity in order to keep his emotions as much as possible to himself. An enormous amount of dishonest nonsense has been and will be written by uncreative critics, of course in the higher interests of crea tive authors, about popularity and the proper attitude of the artist thereto. But possibly the attitude of a first-class artist himself may prove a more valuable guide.

The *Letters of George Meredith* (of which the first volume is a magnificent unfolding of the character of a great man) are full of references to popularity, references overt and covert. Meredith could never—and quite naturally—get away from the idea of popularity. He was a student of the English public, and could occasionally be unjust to it. Writing to

M. André Raffalovich (who had sent him a letter of appreciation) in November, 1881, he said: "I venture to judge by your name that you are at most but half English. I can consequently believe in the feeling you express for the work of an unpopular writer. Otherwise one would incline to be sceptical, for the English are given to practical jokes, and to stir up the vanity of authors who are supposed to languish in the shade amuses them." A remark curiously unfair to the small, faithful band of admirers which Meredith then had. The whole letter, while warmly and touchingly grateful, is gloomy. Further on in it he says: "Good work has a fair chance to be recognised in the end, and if not, what does it matter?" But there is constant proof that it did matter very much. In a letter to William Hardman, written when he was well and hopeful, he says: "Never mind: if we do but get the public ear, oh, my dear old boy!" To Captain Maxse, in reference to a vast sum of £8,000 paid by the *Cornhill* people to George Eliot (for an unreadable novel), he exclaims: "Bon Dieu! Will aught like this ever happen to me?"

And to his son he was very explicit about the extent to which unpopularity "mattered": "As I am unpopular I am ill-paid, and therefore bound to work double tides, hardly ever able to lay down the pen. This affects my weakened stomach, and so the round of the vicious circle is looped." (Vol. I., p. 322.) And in another letter to Arthur Meredith about the same time he sums up his career thus: "As for me, I have failed, and I find little to make the end undesirable." (Vol. I., p. 318.) This letter is dated June 23rd, 1881. Meredith was then fifty-three years of age. He had written *Modern Love*, *The Shaving of Shagpat*, *The Ordeal of Richard Feverel*, *Rhoda Fleming*, *The Egoist* and other masterpieces. He knew that he had done his best and that his best was very fine. It would be difficult to credit that he did not privately deem himself one of the masters of English literature and destined to what we call immortality. He had the enthusiastic appreciation of some of the finest minds of the epoch. And yet, "As for me, I have failed, and I find little to make the end undesirable." But he had not failed in his industry, nor in the quality of his work, nor in achieving self-respect and the respect of his friends. He had failed only in one thing—immediate popularity.

* * * * *

II

Assuming then that an author is justified in desiring immediate popularity, instead of being content with poverty and the unheard plaudits of posterity, another point presents itself. Ought he to limit himself to a mere desire for popularity, or ought he actually to do something, or to refrain from doing something, to the special end of obtaining popularity? Ought he to say: "I shall write exactly what and how I like, without any regard for the public; I shall consider nothing but my own individuality and powers; I shall be guided solely by my own personal conception of what the public ought to like"? Or ought he to say: "Let me examine this public, and let me see whether some compromise between us is not possible"?

Certain authors are never under the necessity of facing the alternative. Occasionally, by chance, a genius may be so fortunately constituted and so brilliantly endowed that he captures the public at once, prestige being established, and the question of compromise never arises. But this is exceedingly rare. On the other hand, many mediocre authors, exercising the most complete sincerity, find ample appreciation in the vast mediocrity of the public, and are never troubled by any problem worse than the vagaries of their fountain-pens. Such authors enjoy in plenty the gewgaw known as happiness. Of nearly all really original artists, however, it may be said that they are at loggerheads with the public—as an almost inevitable consequence of their originality; and for them the problem of compromise or no-compromise acutely exists.

George Meredith was such an artist. George Meredith before anything else was a poet. He would have been a better poet than a novelist, and I believe that he thought so. The public did not care for his poetry. If he had belonged to the no-compromise school, whose adherents usually have the effrontery to claim him, he would have said: "I shall keep on writing poetry, even if I have to become a stockbroker in order to do it." But when he was only thirty-three—a boy, as authors go—he had already tired of no-compromise. He wrote to Augustus Jessopp: "It may be that in a year or two I shall find time for a full sustained Song . . . The worst is that having taken to prose delineations of character and life, one's affections are divided . . . And in truth, being a servant of the public, *I must wait till my master commands before I take seriously to singing.*" (Vol. I., p. 45.) Here is as good an example as one is likely to find of a first-class artist openly admitting the futility of writing what will not be immediately read, when he can write something else, less to his taste, that will be read. The same sentiment has actuated an immense number of first-class creative artists, including Shakspere, who would have been a rare client for a literary agent . . . So much for refraining from doing the precise sort of work one would prefer to do because it is not appreciated by the public.

There remains the doing of a sort of work against the grain because the public appreciates it—otherwise the pot-boiler. In 1861 Meredith wrote to Mrs Ross: "I am engaged in extra potboiling work which enables me to do this," i.e., to write an occasional long poem. (Vol. I., p. 52.) Oh, base compromise! Seventeen years later he wrote to R.L. Stevenson: "Of potboilers let none speak. Jove hangs them upon necks that could soar above his heights but for the accursed weight." (Vol. I., p. 291.) It may be said that Meredith was forced to write potboilers. He was no more forced to write potboilers than any other author. Sooner than wallow in that shame, he might have earned money in more difficult ways. Or he might have indulged in that starvation so heartily prescribed for authors by a plutocratic noble who occasionally deigns to employ the English tongue in prose. Meredith subdued his muse, and Meredith wrote potboilers, because he was a first-class artist and a man of profound common sense. Being extremely creative, he had to arrive somehow, and he remembered that the earth is the earth, and the world the world, and men men, and he arrived as best he could. The great majority of his peers have acted similarly.

The truth is that an artist who demands appreciation from the public on his own terms, and on none but his own terms, is either a god or a conceited and impractical fool. And he is somewhat more likely to be the latter than the former. He wants too much. There are two sides to every bargain, including the artistic. The most fertile and the most powerful artists are the readiest to recognise this, because their sense of proportion, which is the sense of order, is well developed. The lack of the sense of proportion is the mark of the *petit maître*. The sagacious artist, while respecting himself, will respect the idiosyncrasies of his public. To do both simultaneously is quite possible. In particular, the sagacious artist will respect basic national prejudices. For example, no first-class English novelist or dramatist would dream of allowing to his pen the freedom in treating sexual phenomena which Continental writers enjoy as a matter of course. The British public is admittedly wrong on this important point—hypocritical, illogical and absurd. But what would you? You cannot defy it; you literally cannot. If you tried, you would not even get as far as print, to say nothing of library counters. You can only get round it by ingenuity and guile. You can only go a very little further than is quite safe. You can only do one man's modest share in the education of the public.

In Valery Larbaud's latest novel, *A.O. Barnabooth,* occurs a phrase of deep wisdom about women: *"La femme est une grande realite, comme la guerre."* It might be applied to the public. The public is a great actuality, like war. If you are a creative and creating artist, you cannot ignore it, though it can ignore you. There it is! You can do something with it, but not much. And what you do not do with it, it must do with you, if there is to be the contact which is essential to the artistic function. This contact may be closened and completed by the artist's cleverness—the mere cleverness of adaptability which most first-class artists have exhibited. You can wear the fashions of the day. You can tickle the ingenuous beast's ear in order to distract his attention while you stab him in the chest. You can cajole money out of him by one kind of work in order to gain leisure in which to force him to accept later on something that he would prefer to refuse. You can use a thousand devices on the excellent simpleton . . . And in the process you may degrade your self to a mere popularity-hunter! Of course you may; as you may become a drunkard through drinking a glass of beer. Only, if you have anything to say worth saying, you usually don't succumb to this danger. If you have anything to say worth saying, you usually manage somehow to get it said, and read. The artist of genuine vocation is apt to be a wily person. He knows how to sacrifice inessentials so that he may retain essentials. And he can mysteriously put himself even into a potboiler. *Clarissa Harlowe*, which influenced fiction throughout Europe, was the direct result of potboiling. If the artist has not the wit and the strength of mind to keep his own soul amid the collisions of life, he is the inferior of a plain, honest merchant in stamina, and ought to retire to the upper branches of the Civil Service.

* * * * *

III

When the author has finished the composition of a work, when he has put into the trappings of the time as much of his eternal self as they will safely hold, having regard to the best welfare of his creative career as a whole, when, in short, he has done all that he can to ensure the fullest public appreciation of the essential in him—there still remains to be accomplished something which is not unimportant in the entire affair of obtaining contact with the public. He has to see that the work is placed before the public as advantageously as possible. In other words, he has to dispose of the work as advantageously as possible. In other words, when he lays down the pen he ought to become a merchant, for the mere reason that he has an article to sell, and the more skilfully he sells it the better will be the result, not only for the public appreciation of his message, but for himself as a private individual and as an artist with further activities in front of him.

Now this absolutely logical attitude of a merchant towards one's finished work infuriates the dilettanti of the literary world, to whom the very word "royalties" is anathema. They apparently would prefer to treat literature as they imagine Byron treated it, although as a fact no poet in a short life ever contrived to make as many pounds sterling out of verse as Byron made. Or perhaps they would like to return to the golden days when the author had to be "patronised" in order to exist; or even to the mid-nineteenth century, when practically all authors save the most successful—and not a few of the successful also—failed to obtain the fair reward of their work. The dilettanti's snobbishness and sentimentality prevent them from admitting that, in a democratic age, when an author is genuinely appreciated, either he makes money or he is the foolish victim of a scoundrel. They are fond of saying that agreements and royalties have nothing to do with literature. But agreements and royalties have a very great deal to do with literature. Full contact between artist and public depends largely upon publisher or manager being compelled to be efficient and just. And upon the publisher's or manager's efficiency and justice depend also the dignity, the leisure, the easy flow of coin, the freedom, and the pride which are helpful to the full fruition of any artist. No artist was ever assisted in his career by the yoke, by servitude, by enforced monotony, by overwork, by economic inferiority. See Meredith's correspondence everywhere.

Nor can there be any satisfaction in doing badly that which might be done well. If an artist writes a fine poem, shows it to his dearest friend, and burns it—I can respect him. But if an artist writes a fine poem, and then by sloppiness and snobbishness allows it to be inefficiently published, and fails to secure his own interests in the transaction, on the plea that he is an artist and not a merchant, then I refuse to respect him. A man cannot fulfil, and has no right to fulfil, one function only in this complex world. Some, indeed many, of the greatest creative artists have managed to be very good merchants also, and have not been ashamed of the double *rôle*. To read the correspondence and memoirs of certain supreme artists one might be excused for thinking, indeed, that they were more interested in the *rôle* of merchant than in the other *rôle* ; and yet their work in no wise suffered. In the distribution of energy between the two *rôles* common sense is naturally needed. But the artist who has enough common sense— or, otherwise expressed, enough sense of reality—not to disdain the *rôle* of merchant will probably have enough not to exaggerate it. He may be reassured on one point—namely, that success in the *rôle* of merchant will never impair any self-satisfaction he may feel in the *rôle* of artist. The late discovery of a large public in America delighted Meredith and had a tonic effect on his whole system. It is often hinted, even if it is not often said, that great popularity ought to disturb the conscience of the artist. I do not believe it. If the conscience of the artist is not disturbed during the actual work itself, no subsequent phenomenon will or should disturb it. Once the artist is convinced of his artistic honesty, no public can be too large for his peace of mind. On the other hand, failure in the *rôle* of merchant will emphatically impair his self-satisfaction in the *rôle* of artist and his courage in the further pursuance of that *rôle*.

But many artists have admittedly no aptitude for merchantry. Not only is their sense of the bindingness of a bargain imperfect, but they are apt in business to behave in a puerile manner, to close an arrangement out of mere impatience, to be grossly undiplomatic, to be victimised by their vanity, to believe what they ought not to believe, to discredit what is patently true, to worry over negligible trifles, and generally to make a clumsy mess of their affairs. An artist may say: "I cannot work unless I have a free mind, and I cannot have a free mind if I am to be bothered all the time by details of business."

Apart from the fact that no artist who pretends also to be a man can in this world hope for a free mind, and that if he seeks it by neglecting his debtors he will be deprived of it by his creditors—apart from that, the artist's demand for a free mind is reasonable. Moreover, it is always a distressing sight to see a man trying to do what nature has not fitted him to do, and so doing it ill. Such artists, however—and they form possibly the majority—can always employ an expert to do their business for them, to cope on their behalf with the necessary middleman. Not that I deem the publisher or the theatrical manager to be by nature less upright than any other class of merchant. But the publisher and the theatrical manager have been subjected for centuries to a special and grave temptation. The ordinary merchant deals with other merchants—his equals in business skill. The publisher and the theatrical manager deal with what amounts to a race of children, of whom even arch-angels could not refrain from taking advantage.

When the democratisation of literature seriously set in, it inevitably grew plain that the publisher and the theatrical manager had very humanly been giving way to the temptation with which heaven in her infinite wisdom had pleased to afflict them,—and the Society of Authors came into being. A natural consequence of the general awakening was the self-invention of the literary agent. The Society of Authors, against immense obstacles, has performed wonders in the economic education of the creative artist, and therefore in the improvement of letters. The literary agent, against obstacles still more immense, has carried out the details of the revolution. The outcry—partly sentimental, partly snobbish, but mainly interested—was at first tremendous against these meddlers who would destroy the charming personal relations that used to exist between, for example, the author and the publisher. (The less said about those charming personal relations the better. Documents exist.) But the main battle is now over, and everyone concerned is beautifully aware who holds the field. Though much remains to be done, much has been done; and today the creative artist who, conscious of inability to transact his own affairs efficiently, does not obtain efficient advice and help therein, stands in his own light both as an artist and as a man, and is a reactionary force. He owes the practice of elementary common sense to himself, to his work, and to his profession at large.

* * * * *

IV

The same dilettante spirit which refuses to see the connection between art and money has also a tendency to repudiate the world of men at large, as being unfit for the habitation of artists. This is a still more serious error of attitude—especially in a storyteller. No artist is likely to be entirely admirable who is not a man before he is an artist. The notion that art is first and the rest of the universe nowhere is bound to lead to preciosity and futility in art. The artist who is too sensitive for contacts with the non-artistic world is thereby too sensitive for his vocation, and fit only to fall into gentle ecstasies over the work of artists less sensitive than himself.

The classic modern example of the tragedy of the artist who repudiates the world is Flaubert. At an early age Flaubert convinced himself that he had no use for the world of men. He demanded to be left in solitude and tranquillity. The morbid streak in his constitution grew rapidly under the fostering influences of peace and tranquillity. He was brilliantly peculiar as a schoolboy. As an old man of twenty-two, mourning over the vanished brio of youth, he carried morbidity to perfection. Only when he was travelling (as, for example, in Egypt) do his letters lose for a time their distemper. His love-letters are often ignobly inept, and nearly always spoilt by the crass provincialism of the refined and cultivated hermit. His mistress was a woman difficult to handle and indeed a Tartar in egotism, but as the recipient of Flaubert's love-letters she must win universal sympathy.

Full of a grievance against the whole modern planet, Flaubert turned passionately to ancient times (in which he would have been equally unhappy had he lived in them), and hoped to resurrect beauty when he had failed to see it round about him. Whether or not he did resurrect beauty is a point which the present age is now deciding. His fictions of modern life undoubtedly suffer from his detestation of the material; but considering his manner of existence it is marvellous that he should have been able to accomplish any of them, except *Un Coeur Simple*. The final one, *Bouvard et Pécuchet*, shows the lack of the sense of reality which must be the inevitable sequel of divorce from mankind. It is realism without conviction. No such characters as Bouvard and Pecuchet could ever have existed outside Flaubert's brain, and the reader's resultant impression is that the author has ruined a central idea which was well suited for a grand larkish extravaganza in the hands of a French Swift. But the spectacle of Flaubert writing in *mots justes* a grand larkish extravaganza cannot be conjured up by fancy.

There are many sub-Flauberts rife in London. They are usually more critical than creative, but their influence upon creators, and especially the younger creators, is not negligible. Their aim in preciosity would seem to be to keep themselves unspotted from the world. They are for ever being surprised and hurt by the crudity and coarseness of human nature, and for ever bracing themselves to be not as others are. They would have incurred the anger of Dr. Johnson, and a just discipline for them would be that they should be cross-examined by the great bully in presence of a jury of butchers and sentenced accordingly. The morbid Flaubertian shrinking from reality is to be found to-day even in relatively robust minds. I was recently at a provincial cinema, and witnessed on the screen with a friend a wondrously ingenuous drama entitled "Gold is not All." My friend, who combines the callings of engineer and general adventurer with that of serving his country, leaned over to me in the darkness amid the violent applause, and said: "You know, this kind of thing always makes me ashamed of human nature." I answered him as Johnsonially as the circumstances would allow. Had he lived to the age of fifty so blind that it needed a cinema audience to show him what the general level of human nature really is? Nobody has any right to be ashamed of human nature. Is one ashamed of one's mother? Is one ashamed of the cosmic process of evolution? Human nature *is*. And the more deeply the creative artist, by frank contacts, absorbs that supreme fact into his brain, the better for his work.

There is a numerous band of persons in London—and the novelist and dramatist are not infrequently drawn into their circle—who spend so much time and emotion in practising the rites of the religion of art that they become incapable of real existence. Each is a Stylites on a pillar. Their opinion on Leon Bakst, Francis Thompson, Augustus John, Cyril Scott, Maurice Ravel, Vuillard, James Stephens, E.A. Rickards, Richard Strauss, Eugen d'Albert, etc., may not be without value, and their genuine feverish morbid interest in art has its usefulness; but they know no more about reality than a Pekinese dog on a cushion. They never approach normal life. They scorn it. They have a horror of it. They class politics with the differential calculus. They have heard of Lloyd George, the rise in the price of commodities, and the eternal enigma, what is a sardine; but only because they must open a newspaper to look at the advertisements and announcements relating to the arts. The occasional frequenting of this circle may not be disadvantageous to the creative artist. But let him keep himself inoculated against its disease by constant steady plunges into the cold sea of the general national life. Let him mingle with the public, for God's sake! No phenomenon on this wretched planet, which after all is ours, is meet for the artist's shrinking scorn. And the average man, as to whom the artist's ignorance is often astounding, must for ever constitute the main part of the material in which he works.

Above all, let not the creative artist suppose that the antidote to the circle of dilettantism is the circle of social reform. It is not. I referred in the first chapter to the prevalent illusion that the republic has just now arrived at a crisis, and that if something is not immediately done disaster will soon be upon us. This is the illusion to which the circle of social reforms is naturally prone, and it is an illusion against which the common sense of the creative artist must mightily protest. The world is, without doubt, a very bad world; but it is also a very good world. The function of the artist is certainly concerned more with what is than with what ought to be. When all necessary reform has been accomplished our perfected planet will be stone-cold. Until then the artist's affair is to keep his balance amid warring points of view, and in the main to record and enjoy what is . . . But is not the Minimum Wage Bill urgent? But when the minimum wage is as trite as the jury-system, the urgency of reform will still be tempting the artist too far out of his true path. And the artist who yields is lost.

LITERARY TASTE

HOW TO FORM IT
WITH DETAILED INSTRUCTIONS FOR
COLLECTING A COMPLETE LIBRARY OF
ENGLISH LITERATURE

* * * * *

CHAPTER I

THE AIM

At the beginning a misconception must be removed from the path. Many people, if not most, look on literary taste as an elegant accomplishment, by acquiring which they will complete themselves, and make themselves finally fit as members of a correct society. They are secretly ashamed of their ignorance of literature, in the same way as they would be ashamed of their ignorance of etiquette at a high entertainment, or of their inability to ride a horse if suddenly called upon to do so. There are certain things that a man ought to know, or to know about, and literature is one of them: such is their idea. They have learnt to dress themselves with propriety, and to behave with propriety on all occasions; they are fairly "up" in the questions of the day; by industry and enterprise they are succeeding in their vocations; it behoves them, then, not to forget that an acquaintance with literature is an indispensable part of a self-respecting man's personal baggage. Painting doesn't matter; music doesn't matter very much. But "everyone is supposed to know" about literature. Then, literature is such a charming distraction! Literary taste thus serves two purposes: as a certificate of correct culture and as a private pastime. A young professor of mathematics, immense at mathematics and games, dangerous at chess, capable of Haydn on the violin, once said to me, after listening to some chat on books, "Yes, I must take up literature." As though saying: "I was rather forgetting literature. However, I've polished off all these other things. I'll have a shy at literature now."

This attitude, or any attitude which resembles it, is wrong. To him who really comprehends what literature is, and what the function of literature is, this attitude is simply ludicrous. It is also fatal to the formation of literary taste. People who regard literary taste simply as an accomplishment, and literature simply as a distraction, will never truly succeed either in acquiring the accomplishment or in using it half-acquired as a distraction; though the one is the most perfect of distractions, and though the other is unsurpassed by any other accomplishment in elegance or in power to impress the universal snobbery of civilised mankind. Literature, instead of being an accessory, is the fundamental *sine qua non* of complete living. I am extremely anxious to avoid rhetorical exaggerations. I do not think I am guilty of one in asserting that he who has not been "presented to the freedom" of literature has not wakened up out of his prenatal sleep. He is merely not born. He can't see; he can't hear; he can't feel, in any full sense. He can only eat his dinner. What more than anything else annoys people who know the true function of literature, and have profited thereby, is the spectacle of so many thousands of individuals going about under the delusion that they are alive, when, as a fact, they are no nearer being alive than a bear in winter.

I will tell you what literature is! No—I only wish I could. But I can't. No one can. Gleams can be thrown on the secret, inklings given, but no more. I will try to give you an inkling. And, to do so, I will take you back into your own history, or forward into it. That evening when you went for a walk with your faithful friend, the friend from whom you hid nothing—or almost nothing . . . ! You were, in truth, somewhat inclined to hide from him the particular matter which monopolised your mind that evening, but somehow you contrived to get on to it, drawn by an overpowering fascination. And as your faithful friend was sympathetic and discreet, and flattered you by a respectful curiosity, you proceeded further and further into the said matter, growing more and more confidential, until at last you cried out, in a terrific whisper: "My boy, she is simply miraculous!" At that moment you were in the domain of literature.

Let me explain. Of course, in the ordinary acceptation of the word, she was not miraculous. Your faithful friend had never noticed that she was miraculous, nor had about forty thousand other fairly keen observers. She was just a girl. Troy had not been burnt for her. A girl cannot be called a miracle. If a girl is to be called a miracle, then you might call pretty nearly anything a miracle . . . That is just it: you might. You can. You ought. Amid all the miracles of the universe you had just wakened up to one. You were full of your discovery. You were under a divine impulsion to impart that discovery. You had a strong sense of the marvellous beauty of something, and you had to share it. You were in a passion about something, and you had to vent yourself on somebody. You were drawn towards the whole of the rest of the human race. Mark the effect of your mood and utterance on your faithful friend. He knew that she was not a miracle. No other person could have made him believe that she was a miracle. But you, by the force and sincerity of your own vision of her, and by the fervour of your desire to make him participate in your vision, did for quite a long time cause him to feel that he had been blind to the miracle of that girl.

You were producing literature. You were alive. Your eyes were unlidded, your ears were unstopped, to some part of the beauty and the strangeness of the world; and a strong instinct within you forced you to tell someone. It was not enough for you that you saw and heard. Others had to see and hear. Others had to be wakened up. And they were! It is quite possible—I am not quite sure—that your faithful friend the very next day, or the next month, looked at some other girl, and suddenly saw that she, too, was miraculous! The influence of literature!

The makers of literature are those who have seen and felt the miraculous interestingness of the universe. And the greatest makers of literature are those whose vision has been the widest, and whose feeling has been the most intense. Your own fragment of insight was accidental, and perhaps temporary. *Their* lives are one long ecstasy of denying that the world is a dull place. Is it nothing to you to learn to understand that the world is not a dull place? Is it nothing to you to be led out of the tunnel on to the hillside, to have all your senses quickened, to be invigorated by the true savour of life, to feel your heart beating under that correct necktie of yours? These makers of literature render you their equals.

The aim of literary study is not to amuse the hours of leisure; it is to awake oneself, it is to be alive, to intensify one's capacity for pleasure, for sympathy, and for comprehension. It is not to affect one hour, but twenty-four hours. It is to change utterly one's relations with the world. An understanding appreciation of literature means an understanding appreciation of the world, and it means nothing else. Not isolated and unconnected parts of life, but all of life, brought together and correlated in a synthetic map! The spirit of literature is unifying; it joins the candle and the star, and by the magic of an image shows that the beauty of the greater is in the less. And, not content with the disclosure of beauty and the bringing together of all things whatever within its focus, it enforces a moral wisdom by the tracing everywhere of cause and effect. It consoles doubly—by the revelation of unsuspected loveliness, and by the proof that our lot is the common lot. It is the supreme cry of the discoverer, offering sympathy and asking for it in a single gesture. In attending a University Extension Lecture on the sources of Shakespeare's plots, or in studying the researches of George Saintsbury into the origins of English prosody, or in weighing the evidence for and against the assertion that Rousseau was a scoundrel, one is apt to forget what literature really is and is for. It is well to remind ourselves that literature is first and last a means of life, and that the enterprise of forming one's literary taste is an enterprise of learning how best to use this means of life. People who don't want to live, people who would sooner hibernate than feel intensely, will be wise to eschew literature. They had better, to quote from the finest passage in a fine poem, "sit around and eat blackberries." The sight of a "common bush afire with God" might upset their nerves.

CHAPTER II

YOUR PARTICULAR CASE

The attitude of the average decent person towards the classics of his own tongue is one of distrust—I had almost said, of fear. I will not take the case of Shakespeare, for Shakespeare is "taught" in schools; that is to say, the Board of Education and all authorities pedagogic bind themselves together in a determined effort to make every boy in the land a lifelong enemy of Shakespeare. (It is a mercy they don't "teach" Blake.) I will take, for an example, Sir Thomas Browne, as to whom the average person has no offensive juvenile memories. He is bound to have read somewhere that the style of Sir Thomas Browne is unsurpassed by anything in English literature. One day he sees the *Religio Medici* in a shop-window (or, rather, outside a shop-window, for he would hesitate about entering a bookshop), and he buys it, by way of a mild experiment. He does not expect to be enchanted by it; a profound instinct tells him that Sir Thomas Browne is "not in his line"; and in the result he is even less enchanted than he expected to be. He reads the introduction, and he glances at the first page or two of the work. He sees nothing but words. The work makes no appeal to him whatever. He is surrounded by trees, and cannot perceive the forest. He puts the book away. If Sir Thomas Browne is mentioned, he will say, "Yes, very fine!" with a feeling of pride that he has at any rate bought and inspected Sir Thomas Browne. Deep in his heart is a suspicion that people who get enthusiastic about Sir Thomas Browne are vain and conceited *poseurs*. After a year or so, when he has recovered from the discouragement caused by Sir Thomas Browne, he may, if he is young and hopeful, repeat the experiment with Congreve or Addison. Same sequel! And so on for perhaps a decade, until his commerce with the classics finally expires! That, magazines and newish fiction apart, is the literary history of the average decent person.

And even your case, though you are genuinely preoccupied with thoughts of literature, bears certain disturbing resemblances to the drab case of the average person. You do not approach the classics with gusto—anyhow, not with the same gusto as you would approach a new novel by a modern author who had taken your fancy. You never murmured to yourself, when reading Gibbon's *Decline and Fall* in bed: "Well, I really must read one more chapter before I go to sleep!" Speaking generally, the classics do not afford you a pleasure commensurate with their renown. You peruse them with a sense of duty, a sense of doing the right thing, a sense of "improving yourself," rather than with a sense of gladness. You do not smack your lips; you say: "That is good for me." You make little plans for reading, and then you invent excuses for breaking the plans. Something new, something which is not a classic, will surely draw you away from a classic. It is all very well for you to pretend to agree with the verdict of the elect that *Clarissa Harlowe* is one of the greatest novels in the world—a new Kipling, or even a new number of a magazine, will cause you to neglect *Clarissa Harlowe*, just as though Kipling, etc., could not be kept for a few days without turning sour! So that you have to ordain rules for yourself, as: "I will not read anything else until I have read Richardson, or Gibbon, for an hour each day." Thus proving that you regard a classic as a pill, the swallowing of which merits jam! And the more modern a classic is, the more it resembles the stuff of the year and the less it resembles the classics of the centuries, the more easy and enticing do you find that classic. Hence you are glad that George Eliot, the Brontës, Thackeray, are considered as classics, because you really *do* enjoy them. Your sentiments concerning them approach your sentiments concerning a "rattling good story" in a magazine.

I may have exaggerated—or, on the other hand, I may have understated—the unsatisfactory characteristics of your particular case, but it is probable that in the mirror I hold up you recognise the rough outlines of your likeness. You do not care to admit it; but it is so. You are not content with yourself. The desire to be more truly literary persists in you. You feel that there is something wrong in you, but you cannot put your finger on the spot. Further, you feel that you are a bit of a sham. Something within you continually forces you to exhibit for the classics an enthusiasm which you do not sincerely feel. You even try to persuade yourself that you are enjoying a book, when the next moment you drop it in the middle and forget to resume it. You occasionally buy classical works, and do not read them at all; you practically decide that it is enough to possess them, and that the mere possession of them gives you a *cachet*. The truth is, you are a sham. And your soul is a sea of uneasy remorse. You reflect: "According to what Matthew Arnold says, I ought to be perfectly mad about Wordsworth's *Prelude*. And I am not. Why am I not? Have I got to be learned, to undertake a vast course of study, in order to be perfectly mad about Wordsworth's *Prelude*? Or am I born without the faculty of pure taste in literature, despite my vague longings? I do wish I could smack my lips over Wordsworth's *Prelude* as I did over that splendid story by H.G. Wells, *The Country of the Blind*, in the *Strand Magazine*!" . . . Yes, I am convinced that in your dissatisfied, your diviner moments, you address yourself in these terms. I am convinced that I have diagnosed your symptoms.

Now the enterprise of forming one's literary taste is an agreeable one; if it is not agreeable it cannot succeed. But this does not imply that it is an easy or a brief one. The enterprise of beating Colonel Bogey at golf is an agreeable one, but it means honest and regular work. A fact to be borne in mind always! You are certainly not going to realise your ambition—and so great, so influential an ambition!—by spasmodic and half-hearted effort. You must begin by making up your mind adequately. You must rise to the height of the affair. You must approach a grand undertaking in the grand manner. You ought to mark the day in the calendar as a solemnity.

Human nature is weak, and has need of tricky aids, even in the pursuit of happiness. Time will be necessary to you, and time regularly and sacredly set apart. Many people affirm that they cannot be regular, that regularity numbs them. I think this is true of a very few people, and that in the rest the objection to regularity is merely an attempt to excuse idleness. I am inclined to think that you personally are capable of regularity. And I am sure that if you firmly and constantly devote certain specific hours on certain specific days of the week to this business of forming your literary taste, you will arrive at the goal much sooner. The simple act of resolution will help you. This is the first preliminary.

The second preliminary is to surround yourself with books, to create for yourself a bookish atmosphere. The merely physical side of books is important—more important than it may seem to the inexperienced. Theoretically (save for works of reference), a student has need for but one book at a time. Theoretically, an amateur of literature might develop his taste by expending sixpence a week, or a penny a day, in one sixpenny edition of a classic after another sixpenny edition of a classic, and he might store his library in a hat-box or a biscuit-tin. But in practice he would have to be a monster of resolution to succeed in such conditions. The eye must be flattered; the hand must be flattered; the sense of owning must be flattered. Sacrifices must be made for the acquisition of literature. That which has cost a sacrifice is always endeared. A detailed scheme of buying books will come later, in the light of further knowledge. For the present, buy—buy whatever has received the *imprimatur* of critical authority. Buy without any immediate reference to what you will read. Buy! Surround yourself with volumes, as handsome as you can afford. And for reading, all that I will now particularly enjoin is a general and inclusive tasting, in order to attain a sort of familiarity with the look of "literature in all its branches." A turning over of the pages of a volume of Chambers's *Cyclopædia of English Literature*, the third for preference, may be suggested as an admirable and a diverting exercise. You might mark the authors that flash an appeal to you.

CHAPTER III

WHY A CLASSIC IS A CLASSIC

The large majority of our fellow-citizens care as much about literature as they care about aeroplanes or the programme of the Legislature. They do not ignore it; they are not quite indifferent to it. But their interest in it is faint and perfunctory; or, if their interest happens to be violent, it is spasmodic. Ask the two hundred thousand persons whose enthusiasm made the vogue of a popular novel ten years ago what they think of that novel now, and you will gather that they have utterly forgotten it, and that they would no more dream of reading it again than of reading Bishop Stubbs's *Select Charters*. Probably if they did read it again they would not enjoy it—not because the said novel is a whit worse now than it was ten years ago; not because their taste has improved—but because they have not had sufficient practice to be able to rely on their taste as a means of permanent pleasure. They simply don't know from one day to the next what will please them.

In the face of this one may ask: Why does the great and universal fame of classical authors continue? The answer is that the fame of classical authors is entirely independent of the majority. Do you suppose that if the fame of Shakespeare depended on the man in the street it would survive a fortnight? The fame of classical authors is originally made, and it is maintained, by a passionate few. Even when a first-class author has enjoyed immense success during his lifetime, the majority have never appreciated him so sincerely as they have appreciated second-rate men.

He has always been reinforced by the ardour of the passionate few. And in the case of an author who has emerged into glory after his death the happy sequel has been due solely to the obstinate perseverance of the few. They could not leave him alone; they would not. They kept on savouring him, and talking about him, and buying him, and they generally behaved with such eager zeal, and they were so authoritative and sure of themselves, that at last the majority grew accustomed to the sound of his name and placidly agreed to the proposition that he was a genius; the majority really did not care very much either way.

And it is by the passionate few that the renown of genius is kept alive from one generation to another. These few are always at work. They are always rediscovering genius. Their curiosity and enthusiasm are exhaustless, so that there is little chance of genius being ignored. And, moreover, they are always working either for or against the verdicts of the majority. The majority can make a reputation, but it is too careless to maintain it. If, by accident, the passionate few agree with the majority in a particular instance, they will frequently remind the majority that such and such a reputation has been made, and the majority will idly concur: "Ah, yes. By the way, we must not forget that such and such a reputation exists." Without that persistent memory-jogging the reputation would quickly fall into the oblivion which is death. The passionate few only have their way by reason of the fact that they are genuinely interested in literature, that literature matters to them. They conquer by their obstinacy alone, by their eternal repetition of the same statements. Do you suppose they could prove to the man in the street that Shakespeare was a great artist? The said man would not even understand the terms they employed. But when he is told ten thousand times, and generation after generation, that Shakespeare was a great artist, the said man believes—not by reason, but by faith. And he too repeats that Shakespeare was a great artist, and he buys the complete works of Shakespeare and puts them on his shelves, and he goes to see the marvellous stage-effects which accompany *King Lear* or *Hamlet*, and comes back religiously convinced that Shakespeare was a great artist. All because the passionate few could not keep their admiration of Shakespeare to themselves. This is not cynicism; but truth. And it is important that those who wish to form their literary taste should grasp it.

What causes the passionate few to make such a fuss about literature? There can be only one reply. They find a keen and lasting pleasure in literature. They enjoy literature as some men enjoy beer. The recurrence of this pleasure naturally keeps their interest in literature very much alive. They are for ever making new researches, for ever practising on themselves. They learn to understand themselves. They learn to know what they want. Their taste becomes surer and surer as their experience lengthens. They do not enjoy to-day what will seem tedious to them to-morrow. When they find a book tedious, no amount of popular clatter will persuade them that it is pleasurable; and when they find it pleasurable no chill silence of the street-crowds will affect their conviction that the book is good and permanent. They have faith in themselves. What are the qualities in a book which give keen and lasting pleasure to the passionate few? This is a question so difficult that it has never yet been completely answered. You may talk lightly about truth, insight, knowledge, wisdom, humour, and beauty. But these comfortable words do not really carry you very far, for each of them has to be defined, especially the first and last. It is all very well for Keats in his airy manner to assert that beauty is truth, truth beauty, and that that is all he knows or needs to know. I, for one, need to know a lot more. And I never shall know. Nobody, not even Hazlitt nor Sainte-Beuve, has ever finally explained why he thought a book beautiful. I take the first fine lines that come to hand—

> The woods of Arcady are dead,
> And over is their antique joy—

and I say that those lines are beautiful, because they give me pleasure. But why? No answer! I only know that the passionate few will, broadly, agree with me in deriving this mysterious pleasure from those lines. I am only convinced that the liveliness of our pleasure in those and many other lines by the same author will ultimately cause the majority to believe, by faith, that W.B. Yeats is a genius. The one reassuring aspect of the literary affair is that the passionate few are passionate about the same things. A continuance of interest does, in actual practice, lead ultimately to the same judgments. There is only the difference in width of interest. Some of the passionate few lack catholicity, or, rather, the whole of their interest is confined to one narrow channel; they have none left over. These men help specially to vitalise the reputations of the narrower geniuses: such as Crashaw. But their active predilections never contradict the general verdict of the passionate few; rather they reinforce it.

A classic is a work which gives pleasure to the minority which is intensely and permanently interested in literature. It lives on because the minority, eager to renew the sensation of pleasure, is eternally curious and is therefore engaged in an eternal process of rediscovery. A classic does not survive for any ethical reason. It does not survive because it conforms to certain canons, or because neglect would not kill it. It survives because it is a source of pleasure, and because the passionate few can no more neglect it than a bee can neglect a flower. The passionate few do not read "the right things" because they are right. That is to put the cart before the horse. "The right things" are the right things solely because the passionate few *like* reading them. Hence—and I now arrive at my point—the one primary essential to literary taste is a hot interest in literature. If you have that, all the rest will come. It matters nothing that at present you fail to find pleasure in certain classics. The driving impulse of your interest will force you to acquire experience, and experience will teach you the use of the means of pleasure. You do not know the secret ways of yourself: that is all. A continuance of interest must inevitably bring you to the keenest joys. But, of course, experience may be acquired judiciously or injudiciously, just as Putney may be reached *via* Walham Green or *via* St. Petersburg.

CHAPTER IV

WHERE TO BEGIN

I wish particularly that my readers should not be intimidated by the apparent vastness and complexity of this enterprise of forming the literary taste. It is not so vast nor so complex as it looks. There is no need whatever for the inexperienced enthusiast to confuse and frighten himself with thoughts of "literature in all its branches." Experts and pedagogues (chiefly pedagogues) have, for the purpose of convenience, split literature up into divisions and sub-divisions—such as prose and poetry; or imaginative, philosophic, historical; or elegiac, heroic, lyric; or religious and profane, etc., *ad infinitum*. But the greater truth is that literature is all one—and indivisible. The idea of the unity of literature should be well planted and fostered in the head. All literature is the expression of feeling, of passion, of emotion, caused by a sensation of the interestingness of life. What drives a historian to write history? Nothing but the overwhelming impression made upon him by the survey of past times. He is forced into an attempt to reconstitute the picture for others. If hitherto you have failed to perceive that a historian is a being in strong emotion, trying to convey his emotion to others, read the passage in the *Memoirs* of Gibbon, in which he describes how he finished the *Decline and Fall*. You will probably never again look upon the *Decline and Fall* as a "dry" work.

What applies to history applies to the other "dry" branches. Even Johnson's Dictionary is packed with emotion. Read the last paragraph of the preface to it: "In this work, when it shall be found that much is omitted, let it not be forgotten that much likewise is performed . . . It may repress the triumph of malignant criticism to observe that if our language is not here fully displayed, I have only failed in an attempt which no human powers have hitherto completed . . ." And so on to the close: "I have protracted my work till most of those whom I wish to please have sunk into the grave, and success and miscarriage are empty sounds: I therefore dismiss it with frigid tranquillity, having little to fear or hope from censure or from praise." Yes, tranquillity; but not frigid! The whole passage, one of the finest in English prose, is marked by the heat of emotion. You may discover the same quality in such books as Spencer's *First Principles*. You may discover it everywhere in literature, from the cold fire of Pope's irony to the blasting temperatures of Swinburne. Literature does not begin till emotion has begun.

There is even no essential, definable difference between those two great branches, prose and poetry. For prose may have rhythm. All that can be said is that verse will scan, while prose will not. The difference is purely formal. Very few poets have succeeded in being so poetical as Isaiah, Sir Thomas Browne, and Ruskin have been in prose. It can only be stated that, as a rule, writers have shown an instinctive tendency to choose verse for the expression of the very highest emotion. The supreme literature is in verse, but the finest achievements in prose approach so nearly to the finest achievements in verse that it is ill work deciding between them. In the sense in which poetry is best understood, all literature is poetry—or is, at any rate, poetical in quality. Macaulay's ill-informed and unjust denunciations live because his genuine emotion made them into poetry, while his *Lays of Ancient Rome* are dead because they are not the expression of a genuine emotion. As the literary taste develops, this quality of emotion, restrained or loosed, will be more and more widely perceived at large in literature. It is the quality that must be looked for. It is the quality that unifies literature (and all the arts).

It is not merely useless, it is harmful, for you to map out literature into divisions and branches, with different laws, rules, or canons. The first thing is to obtain some possession of literature. When you have actually felt some of the emotion which great writers have striven to impart to you, and when your emotions become so numerous and puzzling that you feel the need of arranging them and calling them by names, then—and not before—you can begin to study what has been attempted in the way of classifying and ticketing literature. Manuals and treatises are excellent things in their kind, but they are simply dead weight at the start. You can only acquire really useful general ideas by first acquiring particular ideas, and putting those particular ideas together. You cannot make bricks without straw. Do not worry about literature in the abstract, about theories as to literature. Get at it. Get hold of literature in the concrete as a dog gets hold of a bone. If you ask me where you ought to begin, I shall gaze at you as I might gaze at the faithful animal if he inquired which end of the bone he ought to attack. It doesn't matter in the slightest degree where you begin. Begin wherever the fancy takes you to begin. Literature is a whole.

There is only one restriction for you. You must begin with an acknowledged classic; you must eschew modern works. The reason for this does not imply any depreciation of the present age at the expense of past ages. Indeed, it is important, if you wish ultimately to have a wide, catholic taste, to guard against the too common assumption that nothing modern will stand comparison with the classics. In every age there have been people to sigh: "Ah, yes. Fifty years ago we had a few great writers. But they are all dead, and no young ones are arising to take their place." This attitude of mind is deplorable, if not silly, and is a certain proof of narrow taste. It is a surety that in 1959 gloomy and egregious persons will be saying: "Ah, yes. At the beginning of the century there were great poets like Swinburne, Meredith, Francis Thompson, and Yeats. Great novelists like Hardy and Conrad. Great historians like Stubbs and Maitland, etc., etc. But they are all dead now, and whom have we to take their place?" It is not until an age has receded into history, and all its mediocrity has dropped away from it, that we can see it as it is—as a group of men of genius. We forget the immense amount of twaddle that the great epochs produced. The total amount of fine literature created in a given period of time differs from epoch to epoch, but it does not differ much. And we may be perfectly sure that our own age will make a favourable impression upon that excellent judge, posterity. Therefore, beware of disparaging the present in your own mind. While temporarily ignoring it, dwell upon the idea that its chaff contains about as much wheat as any similar quantity of chaff has contained wheat.

The reason why you must avoid modern works at the beginning is simply that you are not in a position to choose among modern works. Nobody at all is quite in a position to choose with certainty among modern works. To sift the wheat from the chaff is a process that takes an exceedingly long time. Modern works have to pass before the bar of the taste of successive generations. Whereas, with classics, which have been through the ordeal, almost the reverse is the case. *Your taste has to pass before the bar of the classics.* That is the point. If you differ with a classic, it is you who are wrong, and not the book. If you differ with a modern work, you may be wrong or you may be right, but no judge is authoritative enough to decide. Your taste is unformed. It needs guidance, and it needs authoritative guidance. Into the business of forming literary taste faith enters. You probably will not specially care for a particular classic at first. If you did care for it at first, your taste, so far as that classic is concerned, would be formed, and our hypothesis is that your taste is not formed. How are you to arrive at the stage of caring for it? Chiefly, of course, by examining it and honestly trying to understand it. But this process is materially helped by an act of faith, by the frame of mind which says: "I know on the highest authority that this thing is fine, that it is capable of giving me pleasure. Hence I am determined to find pleasure in it." Believe me that faith counts enormously in the development of that wide taste which is the instrument of wide pleasures. But it must be faith founded on unassailable authority.

CHAPTER V

HOW TO READ A CLASSIC

Let us begin experimental reading with Charles Lamb. I choose Lamb for various reasons: He is a great writer, wide in his appeal, of a highly sympathetic temperament; and his finest achievements are simple and very short. Moreover, he may usefully lead to other and more complex matters, as will appear later. Now, your natural tendency will be to think of Charles Lamb as a book, because he has arrived at the stage of being a classic. Charles Lamb was a man, not a book. It is extremely important that the beginner in literary study should always form an idea of the man behind the book. The book is nothing but the expression of the man. The book is nothing but the man trying to talk to you, trying to impart to you some of his feelings. An experienced student will divine the man from the book, will understand the man by the book, as is, of course, logically proper. But the beginner will do well to aid himself in understanding the book by means of independent information about the man. He will thus at once relate the book to something human, and strengthen in his mind the essential notion of the connection between literature and life. The earliest literature was delivered orally direct by the artist to the recipient. In some respects this arrangement was ideal. Changes in the constitution of society have rendered it impossible. Nevertheless, we can still, by the exercise of the imagination, hear mentally the accents of the artist speaking to us. We must so exercise our imagination as to feel the man behind the book.

Some biographical information about Lamb should be acquired. There are excellent short biographies of him by Canon Ainger in the *Dictionary of National Biography*, in Chambers's *Encyclopædia*, and in Chambers's *Cyclopædia of English Literature*. If you have none of these (but you ought to have the last), there are Mr. E. V. Lucas's exhaustive *Life* (Methuen, 7s. 6d.), and, cheaper, Mr. Walter Jerrold's *Lamb* (Bell and Sons, 1s.); also introductory studies prefixed to various editions of Lamb's works. Indeed, the facilities for collecting materials for a picture of Charles Lamb as a human being are prodigious. When you have made for yourself such a picture, read the *Essays of Elia* the light of it. I will choose one of the most celebrated, *Dream Children: A Reverie*. At this point, kindly put my book down, and read *Dream Children*. Do not say to yourself that you will read it later, but read it now. When you have read it, you may proceed to my next paragraph.

You are to consider *Dream Children* as a human document. Lamb was nearing fifty when he wrote it. You can see, especially from the last line, that the death of his elder brother, John Lamb, was fresh and heavy on his mind. You will recollect that in youth he had had a disappointing love-affair with a girl named Ann Simmons, who afterwards married a man named Bartrum. You will know that one of the influences of his childhood was his grandmother Field, housekeeper of Blakesware House, in Hertfordshire, at which mansion he sometimes spent his holidays. You will know that he was a bachelor, living with his sister Mary, who was subject to homicidal mania. And you will see in this essay, primarily, a supreme expression of the increasing loneliness of his life. He constructed all that preliminary tableau of paternal pleasure in order to bring home to you in the most poignant way his feeling of the solitude of his existence, his sense of all that he had missed and lost in the world. The key of the essay is one of profound sadness. But note that he makes his sadness beautiful; or, rather, he shows the beauty that resides in sadness. You watch him sitting there in his "bachelor arm-chair," and you say to yourself: "Yes, it was sad, but it was somehow beautiful." When you have said that to yourself, Charles Lamb, so far as you are concerned, has accomplished his chief aim in writing the essay. How exactly he produces his effect can never be fully explained. But one reason of his success is certainly his regard for truth. He does not falsely idealise his brother, nor the relations between them. He does not say, as a sentimentalist would have said, "Not the slightest cloud ever darkened our relations;" nor does he exaggerate his solitude. Being a sane man, he has too much common-sense to assemble all his woes at once. He might have told you that Bridget was a homicidal maniac; what he does tell you is that she was faithful. Another reason of his success is his continual regard for beautiful things and fine actions, as illustrated in the major characteristics of his grandmother and his brother, and in the detailed description of Blakesware House and the gardens thereof.

Then, subordinate to the main purpose, part of the machinery of the main purpose, is the picture of the children—real children until the moment when they fade away. The traits of childhood are accurately and humorously put in again and again: "Here John smiled, as much as to say, 'That would be foolish indeed.'" "Here little Alice spread her hands." "Here Alice's little right foot played an involuntary movement, till, upon my looking grave, it desisted." "Here John expanded all his eyebrows, and tried to look courageous." "Here John slily deposited back upon the plate a bunch of grapes." "Here the children fell a-crying . . . and prayed me to tell them some stories about their pretty dead mother." And the exquisite: "Here Alice put out one of her dear mother's looks, too tender to be upbraiding." Incidentally, while preparing his ultimate solemn effect, Lamb has inspired you with a new, intensified vision of the wistful beauty of children—their imitativeness, their facile and generous emotions, their anxiety to be correct, their ingenuous haste to escape from grief into joy. You can see these children almost as clearly and as tenderly as Lamb saw them. For days afterwards you will not be able to look upon a child without recalling Lamb's portrayal of the grace of childhood. He will have shared with you his perception of beauty. If you possess children, he will have renewed for you the charm which custom does very decidedly stale. It is further to be noticed that the measure of his success in picturing the children is the measure of his success in his main effect. The more real they seem, the more touching is the revelation of the fact that they do not exist, and never have existed. And if you were moved by the reference to their "pretty dead mother," you will be still more moved when you learn that the girl who would have been their mother is not dead and is not Lamb's.

As, having read the essay, you reflect upon it, you will see how its emotional power over you has sprung from the sincere and unexaggerated expression of actual emotions exactly remembered by someone who had an eye always open for beauty, who was, indeed, obsessed by beauty. The beauty of old houses and gardens and aged virtuous characters, the beauty of children, the beauty of companionships, the softening beauty of dreams in an arm-chair—all these are brought together and mingled with the grief and regret which were the origin of the mood. Why is *Dream Children* a classic? It is a classic because it transmits to you, as to generations before you, distinguished emotion, because it makes you respond to the throb of life more intensely, more justly, and more nobly. And it is capable of doing this because Charles Lamb had a very distinguished, a very sensitive, and a very honest mind. His emotions were noble. He felt so keenly that he was obliged to find relief in imparting his emotions. And his mental processes were so sincere that he could neither exaggerate nor diminish the truth. If he had lacked any one of these three qualities, his appeal would have been narrowed and weakened, and he would not have become a classic. Either his feelings would have been deficient in supreme beauty, and therefore less worthy to be imparted, or he would not have had sufficient force to impart them; or his honesty would not have been equal to the strain of imparting them accurately. In any case, he would not have set up in you that vibration which we call pleasure, and which is super-eminently caused by vitalising participation in high emotion. As Lamb sat in his bachelor arm-chair, with his brother in the grave, and the faithful homicidal maniac by his side, he really did think to himself, "This is beautiful. Sorrow is beautiful. Disappointment is beautiful. Life is beautiful. *I must tell them*. I must make them understand." Because he still makes you understand he is a classic. And now I seem to hear you say, "But what about Lamb's famous literary style? Where does that come in?"

CHAPTER VI

THE QUESTION OF STYLE

In discussing the value of particular books, I have heard people say—people who were timid about expressing their views of literature in the presence of literary men: "It may be bad from a literary point of view, but there are very good things in it." Or: "I dare say the style is very bad, but really the book is very interesting and suggestive." Or: "I'm not an expert, and so I never bother my head about good style. All I ask for is good matter. And when I have got it, critics may say what they like about the book." And many other similar remarks, all showing that in the minds of the speakers there existed a notion that style is something supplementary to, and distinguishable from, matter; a sort of notion that a writer who wanted to be classical had first to find and arrange his matter, and then dress it up elegantly in a costume of style, in order to please beings called literary critics.

This is a misapprehension. Style cannot be distinguished from matter. When a writer conceives an idea he conceives it in a form of words. That form of words constitutes his style, and it is absolutely governed by the idea. The idea can only exist in words, and it can only exist in one form of words. You cannot say exactly the same thing in two different ways. Slightly alter the expression, and you slightly alter the idea. Surely it is obvious that the expression cannot be altered without altering the thing expressed! A writer, having conceived and expressed an idea, may, and probably will, "polish it up." But what does he polish up? To say that he polishes up his style is merely to say that he is polishing up his idea, that he has discovered faults or imperfections in his idea, and is perfecting it. An idea exists in proportion as it is expressed; it exists when it is expressed, and not before. It expresses itself. A clear idea is expressed clearly, and a vague idea vaguely. You need but take your own case and your own speech. For just as science is the development of common-sense, so is literature the development of common daily speech. The difference between science and common-sense is simply one of degree; similarly with speech and literature. Well, when you "know what you think," you succeed in saying what you think, in making yourself understood. When you "don't know what to think," your expressive tongue halts. And note how in daily life the characteristics of your style follow your mood; how tender it is when you are tender, how violent when you are violent. You have said to yourself in moments of emotion: "If only I could write—," etc. You were wrong. You ought to have said: "If only I could *think*—on this high plane." When you have thought clearly you have never had any difficulty in saying what you thought, though you may occasionally have had some difficulty in keeping it to yourself. And when you cannot express yourself, depend upon it that you have nothing precise to express, and that what incommodes you is not the vain desire to express, but the vain desire to *think* more clearly. All this just to illustrate how style and matter are co-existent, and inseparable, and alike.

You cannot have good matter with bad style. Examine the point more closely. A man wishes to convey a fine idea to you. He employs a form of words. That form of words is his style. Having read, you say: "Yes, this idea is fine." The writer has therefore achieved his end. But in what imaginable circumstances can you say: "Yes, this idea is fine, but the style is not fine"? The sole medium of communication between you and the author has been the form of words. The fine idea has reached you. How? In the words, by the words. Hence the fineness must be in the words. You may say, superiorly: "He has expressed himself clumsily, but I can *see* what he means." By what light? By something in the words, in the style.

That something is fine. Moreover, if the style is clumsy, are you sure that you can see what he means? You cannot be quite sure. And at any rate, you cannot see distinctly. The "matter" is what actually reaches you, and it must necessarily be affected by the style.

Still further to comprehend what style is, let me ask you to think of a writer's style exactly as you would think of the gestures and manners of an acquaintance. You know the man whose demeanour is "always calm," but whose passions are strong. How do you know that his passions are strong? Because he "gives them away" by some small, but important, part of his demeanour, such as the twitching of a lip or the whitening of the knuckles caused by clenching the hand. In other words, his demeanour, fundamentally, is not calm. You know the man who is always "smoothly polite and agreeable," but who affects you unpleasantly. Why does he affect you unpleasantly? Because he is tedious, and therefore disagreeable, and because his politeness is not real politeness. You know the man who is awkward, shy, clumsy, but who, nevertheless, impresses you with a sense of dignity and force. Why? Because mingled with that awkwardness and so forth *is* dignity. You know the blunt, rough fellow whom you instinctively guess to be affectionate—because there is "something in his tone" or "something in his eyes." In every instance the demeanour, while perhaps seeming to be contrary to the character, is really in accord with it. The demeanour never contradicts the character. It is one part of the character that contradicts another part of the character. For, after all, the blunt man *is* blunt, and the awkward man *is* awkward, and these characteristics are defects. The demeanour merely expresses them. The two men would be better if, while conserving their good qualities, they had the superficial attributes of smoothness and agreeableness possessed by the gentleman who is unpleasant to you. And as regards this latter, it is not his superficial attributes which are unpleasant to you; but his other qualities. In the end the character is shown in the demeanour; and the demeanour is a consequence of the character and resembles the character. So with style and matter. You may argue that the blunt, rough man's demeanour is unfair to his tenderness. I do not think so. For his churlishness is really very trying and painful, even to the man's wife, though a moment's tenderness will make her and you forget it. The man really is churlish, and much more often than he is tender. His demeanour is merely just to his character. So, when a writer annoys you for ten pages and then enchants you for ten lines, you must not explode against his style. You must not say that his style won't let his matter "come out." You must remember the churlish, tender man. The more you reflect, the more clearly you will see that faults and excellences of style are faults and excellences of matter itself.

One of the most striking illustrations of this neglected truth is Thomas Carlyle. How often has it been said that Carlyle's matter is marred by the harshness and the eccentricities of his style? But Carlyle's matter is harsh and eccentric to precisely the same degree as his style is harsh and eccentric. Carlyle was harsh and eccentric. His behaviour was frequently ridiculous, if it were not abominable. His judgments were often extremely bizarre. When you read one of Carlyle's fierce diatribes, you say to yourself: "This is splendid. The man's enthusiasm for justice and truth is glorious." But you also say: "He is a little unjust and a little untruthful. He goes too far. He lashes too hard." These things are not the style; they are the matter. And when, as in his greatest moments, he is emotional and restrained at once, you say: "This is the real Carlyle." Kindly notice how perfect the style has become! No harshnesses or eccentricities now! And if that particular matter is the "real" Carlyle, then that particular style is Carlyle's "real" style. But when you say "real" you would more properly say "best." "This is the best Carlyle." If Carlyle had always been at his best he would have counted among the supreme geniuses of the world. But he was a mixture. His style is the expression of the mixture. The faults are only in the style because they are in the matter.

You will find that, in classical literature, the style always follows the mood of the matter. Thus, Charles Lamb's essay on *Dream Children* begins quite simply, in a calm, narrative manner, enlivened by a certain quippishness concerning the children. The style is grave when great-grandmother Field is the subject, and when the author passes to a rather elaborate impression of the picturesque old mansion it becomes as it were consciously beautiful. This beauty is intensified in the description of the still more beautiful garden. But the real dividing point of the essay occurs when Lamb approaches his elder brother. He unmistakably marks the point with the phrase: "*Then, in somewhat a more heightened tone*, I told how," etc. Henceforward the style increases in fervour and in solemnity until the culmination of the essay is reached: "And while I stood gazing, both the children gradually grew fainter to my view, receding and still receding till nothing at last but two mournful features were seen in the uttermost distance, which, without speech, strangely impressed upon me the effects of speech . . ." Throughout, the style is governed by the matter. "Well," you say, "of course it is. It couldn't be otherwise. If it were otherwise it would be ridiculous. A man who made love as though he were preaching a sermon, or a man who preached a sermon as though he were teasing schoolboys, or a man who described a death as though he were describing a practical joke, must necessarily be either an ass or a lunatic." Just so. You have put it in a nutshell. You have disposed of the problem of style so far as it can be disposed of.

But what do those people mean who say: "I read such and such an author for the beauty of his style alone"? Personally, I do not clearly know what they mean (and I have never been able to get them to explain), unless they mean that they read for the beauty of sound alone. When you read a book there are only three things of which you may be conscious: (1) The significance of the words, which is inseparably bound up with the thought. (2) The look of the printed words on the page—I do not suppose that anybody reads any author for the visual beauty of the words on the page. (3) The sound of the words, either actually uttered or imagined by the brain to be uttered. Now it is indubitable that words differ in beauty of sound. To my mind one of the most beautiful words in the English language is "pavement." Enunciate it, study its sound, and see what you think. It is also indubitable that certain combinations of words have a more beautiful sound than certain other combinations. Thus Tennyson held that the most beautiful line he ever wrote was:

The mellow ouzel fluting in the elm.

Perhaps, as sound, it was. Assuredly it makes a beautiful succession of sounds, and recalls the bird-sounds which it is intended to describe. But does it live in the memory as one of the rare great Tennysonian lines? It does not. It has charm, but the charm is merely curious or pretty. A whole poem composed of lines with no better recommendation than that line has would remain merely curious or pretty. It would not permanently interest. It would be as insipid as a pretty woman who had nothing behind her prettiness. It would not live. One may remark in this connection how the merely verbal felicities of Tennyson have lost our esteem. Who will now proclaim the *Idylls of the King* as a masterpiece? Of the thousands of lines written by him which please the ear, only those survive of which the matter is charged with emotion. No! As regards the man who professes to read an author "for his style alone," I am inclined to think either that he will soon get sick of that author, or that he is deceiving himself and means the author's general temperament—not the author's verbal style, but a peculiar quality which runs through all the matter written by the author. Just as one may like a man for something which is always coming out of him, which one cannot define, and which is of the very essence of the man.

In judging the style of an author, you must employ the same canons as you use in judging men. If you do this you will not be tempted to attach importance to trifles that are negligible. There can be no lasting friendship without respect. If an author's style is such that you cannot *respect* it, then you may be sure that, despite any present pleasure which you may obtain from that author, there is something wrong with his matter, and that the pleasure will soon cloy. You must examine your sentiments towards an author. If when you have read an author you are pleased, without being conscious of aught but his mellifluousness, just conceive what your feelings would be after spending a month's holiday with a merely mellifluous man. If an author's style has pleased you, but done nothing except make you giggle, then reflect upon the ultimate tediousness of the man who can do nothing but jest. On the other hand, if you are impressed by what an author has said to you, but are aware of verbal clumsinesses in his work, you need worry about his "bad style" exactly as much and exactly as little as you would worry about the manners of a kindhearted, keen-brained friend who was dangerous to carpets with a tea-cup in his hand. The friend's antics in a drawing-room are somewhat regrettable, but you would not say of him that his manners were bad. Again, if an author's style dazzles you instantly and blinds you to everything except its brilliant self, ask your soul, before you begin to admire his matter, what would be your final opinion of a man who at the first meeting fired his personality into you like a broadside. Reflect that, as a rule, the people whom you have come to esteem communicated themselves to you gradually, that they did not begin the entertainment with fireworks. In short, look at literature as you would look at life, and you cannot fail to perceive that, essentially, the style is the man. Decidedly you will never assert that you care nothing for style, that your enjoyment of an author's matter is unaffected by his style. And you will never assert, either, that style alone suffices for you.

If you are undecided upon a question of style, whether leaning to the favourable or to the unfavourable, the most prudent course is to forget that literary style exists. For, indeed, as style is understood by most people who have not analysed their impressions under the influence of literature, there *is* no such thing as literary style. You cannot divide literature into two elements and say: This is matter and that style. Further, the significance and the worth of literature are to be comprehended and assessed in the same way as the significance and the worth of any other phenomenon: by the exercise of common-sense. Common-sense will tell you that nobody, not even a genius, can be simultaneously vulgar and distinguished, or beautiful and ugly, or precise and vague, or tender and harsh. And common-sense will therefore tell you that to try to set up vital contradictions between matter and style is absurd. When there is a superficial contradiction, one of the two mutually-contradicting qualities is of far less importance than the other. If you refer literature to the standards of life, common-sense will at once decide which quality should count heaviest in your esteem. You will be in no danger of weighing a mere maladroitness of manner against a fine trait of character, or of letting a graceful deportment blind you to a fundamental vacuity. When in doubt, ignore style, and think of the matter as you would think of an individual.

CHAPTER VII

WRESTLING WITH AN AUTHOR

Having disposed, so far as is possible and necessary, of that formidable question of style, let us now return to Charles Lamb, whose essay on *Dream Children* was the originating cause of our inquiry into style. As we have made a beginning of Lamb, it will be well to make an end of him. In the preliminary stages of literary culture, nothing is more helpful, in the way of kindling an interest and keeping it well alight, than to specialise for a time on one author, and particularly on an author so frankly and curiously "human" as Lamb is. I do not mean that you should imprison yourself with Lamb's complete works for three months, and read nothing else. I mean that you should regularly devote a proportion of your learned leisure to the study of Lamb until you are acquainted with all that is important in his work and about his work. (You may buy the complete works in prose and verse of Charles and Mary Lamb, edited by that unsurpassed expert Mr. Thomas Hutchison, and published by the Oxford University Press, in two volumes for four shillings the pair!) There is no reason why you should not become a modest specialist in Lamb. He is the very man for you; neither voluminous, nor difficult, nor uncomfortably lofty; always either amusing or touching; and—most important—himself passionately addicted to literature. You cannot like Lamb without liking literature in general. And you cannot read Lamb without learning about literature in general; for books were his hobby, and he was a critic of the first rank. His letters are full of literariness. You will naturally read his letters; you should not only be infinitely diverted by them (there are no better epistles), but you should receive from them much light on the works.

It is a course of study that I am suggesting to you. It means a certain amount of sustained effort. It means slightly more resolution, more pertinacity, and more expenditure of brain-tissue than are required for reading a newspaper. It means, in fact, "work." Perhaps you did not bargain for work when you joined me. But I do not think that the literary taste can be satisfactorily formed unless one is prepared to put one's back into the affair. And I may prophesy to you, by way of encouragement, that, in addition to the advantages of familiarity with masterpieces, of increased literary knowledge, and of a wide introduction to the true bookish atmosphere and "feel" of things, which you will derive from a comprehensive study of Charles Lamb, you will also be conscious of a moral advantage—the very important and very inspiring advantage of really "knowing something about something." You will have achieved a definite step; you will be proudly aware that you have put yourself in a position to judge as an expert whatever you may hear or read in the future concerning Charles Lamb. This legitimate pride and sense of accomplishment will stimulate you to go on further; it will generate steam. I consider that this indirect moral advantage even outweighs, for the moment, the direct literary advantages.

Now, I shall not shut my eyes to a possible result of your diligent intercourse with Charles Lamb. It is possible that you may be disappointed with him. It is—shall I say?—almost probable that you will be disappointed with him, at any rate partially. You will have expected more joy in him than you have received. I have referred in a previous chapter to the feeling of disappointment which often comes from first contacts with the classics. The neophyte is apt to find them—I may as well out with the word—dull. You may have found Lamb less diverting, less interesting, than you hoped. You may have had to whip yourself up again and again to the effort of reading him. In brief, Lamb has not, for you, justified his terrific reputation. If a classic is a classic because it gives *pleasure* to succeeding generations of the people who are most keenly interested in literature, and if Lamb frequently strikes you as dull, then evidently there is something wrong. The difficulty must be fairly fronted, and the fronting of it brings us to the very core of the business of actually forming the taste. If your taste were classical you would discover in Lamb a continual fascination; whereas what you in fact do discover in Lamb is a not unpleasant flatness, enlivened by a vague humour and an occasional pathos. You ought, according to theory, to be enthusiastic; but you are apathetic, or, at best, half-hearted. There is a gulf. How to cross it?

To cross it needs time and needs trouble. The following considerations may aid. In the first place, we have to remember that, in coming into the society of the classics in general and of Charles Lamb in particular, we are coming into the society of a mental superior. What happens usually in such a case? We can judge by recalling what happens when we are in the society of a mental inferior. We say things of which he misses the import; we joke, and he does not smile; what makes him laugh loudly seems to us horseplay or childish; he is blind to beauties which ravish us; he is ecstatic over what strikes us as crude; and his profound truths are for us trite commonplaces. His perceptions are relatively coarse; our perceptions are relatively subtle. We try to make him understand, to make him see, and if he is aware of his inferiority we may have some success. But if he is not aware of his inferiority, we soon hold our tongues and leave him alone in his self-satisfaction, convinced that there is nothing to be done with him. Every one of us has been through this experience with a mental inferior, for there is always a mental inferior handy, just as there is always a being more unhappy than we are. In approaching a classic, the true wisdom is to place ourselves in the position of the mental inferior, aware of mental inferiority, humbly stripping off all conceit, anxious to rise out of that inferiority. Recollect that we always regard as quite hopeless the mental inferior who does not suspect his own inferiority. Our attitude towards

Lamb must be: "Charles Lamb was a greater man than I am, cleverer, sharper, subtler, finer, intellectually more powerful, and with keener eyes for beauty. I must brace myself to follow his lead." Our attitude must resemble that of one who cocks his ear and listens with all his soul for a distant sound.

To catch the sound we really must listen. That is to say, we must read carefully, with our faculties on the watch. We must read slowly and perseveringly. A classic has to be wooed and is worth the wooing. Further, we must disdain no assistance. I am not in favour of studying criticism of classics before the classics themselves. My notion is to study the work and the biography of a classical writer together, and then to read criticism afterwards. I think that in reprints of the classics the customary "critical introduction" ought to be put at the end, and not at the beginning, of the book. The classic should be allowed to make his own impression, however faint, on the virginal mind of the reader. But afterwards let explanatory criticism be read as much as you please. Explanatory criticism is very useful; nearly as useful as pondering for oneself on what one has read! Explanatory criticism may throw one single gleam that lights up the entire subject.

My second consideration (in aid of crossing the gulf) touches the quality of the pleasure to be derived from a classic. It is never a violent pleasure. It is subtle, and it will wax in intensity, but the idea of violence is foreign to it. The artistic pleasures of an uncultivated mind are generally violent. They proceed from exaggeration in treatment, from a lack of balance, from attaching too great an importance to one aspect (usually superficial), while quite ignoring another. They are gross, like the joy of Worcester sauce on the palate. Now, if there is one point common to all classics, it is the absence of exaggeration. The balanced sanity of a great mind makes impossible exaggeration, and, therefore, distortion. The beauty of a classic is not at all apt to knock you down. It will steal over you, rather. Many serious students are, I am convinced, discouraged in the early stages because they are expecting a wrong kind of pleasure. They have abandoned Worcester sauce, and they miss it. They miss the coarse *tang*. They must realise that indulgence in the *tang* means the sure and total loss of sensitiveness—sensitiveness even to the *tang* itself. They cannot have crudeness and fineness together. They must choose, remembering that while crudeness kills pleasure, fineness ever intensifies it.

CHAPTER VIII

SYSTEM IN HEADING

You have now definitely set sail on the sea of literature. You are afloat, and your anchor is up. I think I have given adequate warning of the dangers and disappointments which await the unwary and the sanguine. The enterprise in which you are engaged is not facile, nor is it short. I think I have sufficiently predicted that you will have your hours of woe, during which you may be inclined to send to perdition all writers, together with the inventor of printing. But if you have become really friendly with Lamb; if you know Lamb, or even half of him; if you have formed an image of him in your mind, and can, as it were, hear him brilliantly stuttering while you read his essays or letters, then certainly you are in a fit condition to proceed and you want to know in which direction you are to proceed. Yes, I have caught your terrified and protesting whisper: "I hope to heaven he isn't going to prescribe a Course of English Literature, because I feel I shall never be able to do it!" I am not. If your object in life was to be a University Extension Lecturer in English literature, then I should prescribe something drastic and desolating. But as your object, so far as I am concerned, is simply to obtain the highest and most tonic form of artistic pleasure of which you are capable, I shall not prescribe any regular course. Nay, I shall venture to dissuade you from any regular course. No man, and assuredly no beginner, can possibly pursue a historical course of literature without wasting a lot of weary time in acquiring mere knowledge which will yield neither pleasure nor advantage. In the choice of reading the individual must count; caprice must count, for caprice is often the truest index to the individuality. Stand defiantly on your own feet, and do not excuse yourself to yourself. You do not exist in order to honour literature by becoming an encyclopædia of literature. Literature exists for your service. Wherever you happen to be, that, for you, is the centre of literature.

Still, for your own sake you must confine yourself for a long time to recognised classics, for reasons already explained. And though you should not follow a course, you must have a system or principle. Your native sagacity will tell you that caprice, left quite unfettered, will end by being quite ridiculous. The system which I recommend is embodied in this counsel: Let one thing lead to another. In the sea of literature every part communicates with every other part; there are no land-locked lakes. It was with an eye to this system that I originally recommended you to start with Lamb. Lamb, if you are his intimate, has already brought you into relations with a number of other prominent writers with whom you can in turn be intimate, and who will be particularly useful to you. Among these are Wordsworth, Coleridge, Southey, Hazlitt, and Leigh Hunt. You cannot know Lamb without knowing these men, and some of them are of the highest importance. From the circle of Lamb's own work you may go off at a tangent at various points, according to your inclination. If, for instance, you are drawn towards poetry, you cannot, in all English literature, make a better start than with Wordsworth. And Wordsworth will send you backwards to a comprehension of the poets against whose influence Wordsworth fought. When you have understood Wordsworth's and Coleridge's *Lyrical Ballads*, and Wordsworth's defence of them, you will be in a position to judge poetry in general. If, again, your mind hankers after an earlier and more romantic literature, Lamb's *Specimens of English Dramatic Poets Contemporary with Shakspere* has already, in an enchanting fashion, piloted you into a vast gulf of "the sea which is Shakspere."

Again, in Hazlitt and Leigh Hunt you will discover essayists inferior only to Lamb himself, and critics perhaps not inferior. Hazlitt is unsurpassed as a critic. His judgments are convincing and his enthusiasm of the most catching nature. Having arrived at Hazlitt or Leigh Hunt, you can branch off once more at any one of ten thousand points into still wider circles. And thus you may continue up and down the centuries as far as you like, yea, even to Chaucer. If you chance to read Hazlitt on *Chaucer and Spenser*, you will probably put your hat on instantly and go out and buy these authors; such is his communicating fire! I need not particularise further. Commencing with Lamb, and allowing one thing to lead to another, you cannot fail to be more and more impressed by the peculiar suitability to your needs of the Lamb entourage and the Lamb period. For Lamb lived in a time of universal rebirth in English literature. Wordsworth and Coleridge were re-creating poetry; Scott was re-creating the novel; Lamb was re-creating the human document; and Hazlitt, Coleridge, Leigh Hunt, and others were re-creating criticism. Sparks are flying all about the place, and it will be not less than a miracle if something combustible and indestructible in you does not take fire.

I have only one cautionary word to utter. You may be saying to yourself: "So long as I stick to classics I cannot go wrong." You can go wrong. You can, while reading naught but very fine stuff, commit the grave error of reading too much of one kind of stuff. Now there are two kinds, and only two kinds. These two kinds are not prose and poetry, nor are they divided the one from the other by any differences of form or of subject. They are the inspiring kind and the informing kind. No other genuine division exists in literature. Emerson, I think, first clearly stated it. His terms were the literature of "power" and the literature of "knowledge." In nearly all great literature the two qualities are to be found in company, but one usually predominates over the other. An example of the exclusively inspiring kind is Coleridge's *Kubla Khan*. I cannot recall any first-class example of the purely informing kind. The nearest approach to it that I can name is Spencer's *First Principles*, which, however, is at least once highly inspiring. An example in which the inspiring quality predominates is *Ivanhoe*; and an example in which the informing quality predominates is Hazlitt's essays on Shakespeare's characters. You must avoid giving undue preference to the kind in which the inspiring quality predominates or to the kind in which the informing quality predominates. Too much of the one is enervating; too much of the other is desiccating. If you stick exclusively to the one you may become a mere debauchee of the emotions; if you stick exclusively to the other you may cease to live in any full sense. I do not say that you should hold the balance exactly even between the two kinds. Your taste will come into the scale. What I say is that neither kind must be neglected.

Lamb is an instance of a great writer whom anybody can understand and whom a majority of those who interest themselves in literature can more or less appreciate. He makes no excessive demand either on the intellect or on the faculty of sympathetic emotion. On both sides of Lamb, however, there lie literatures more difficult, more recondite. The "knowledge" side need not detain us here; it can be mastered by concentration and perseverance. But the "power" side, which comprises the supreme productions of genius, demands special consideration. You may have arrived at the point of keenly enjoying Lamb and yet be entirely unable to "see anything in" such writings as *Kubla Khan* or Milton's *Comus*; and as for *Hamlet* you may see nothing in it but a sanguinary tale "full of quotations." Nevertheless it is the supreme productions which are capable of yielding the supreme pleasures, and which *will* yield the supreme pleasures when the pass-key to them has been acquired. This pass-key is a comprehension of the nature of poetry.

CHAPTER IX

VERSE

There is a word, a "name of fear," which rouses terror in the heart of the vast educated majority of the English-speaking race. The most valiant will fly at the mere utterance of that word. The most broad-minded will put their backs up against it. The most rash will not dare to affront it. I myself have seen it empty buildings that had been full; and I know that it will scatter a crowd more quickly than a hose-pipe, hornets, or the rumour of plague. Even to murmur it is to incur solitude, probably disdain, and possibly starvation, as historical examples show. That word is "poetry."

The profound objection of the average man to poetry can scarcely be exaggerated. And when I say the average man, I do not mean the "average sensual man"—any man who gets on to the top of the omnibus; I mean the average lettered man, the average man who does care a little for books and enjoys reading, and knows the classics by name and the popular writers by having read them. I am convinced that not one man in ten who reads, reads poetry—at any rate, knowingly. I am convinced, further, that not one man in ten who goes so far as knowingly to *buy* poetry ever reads it. You will find everywhere men who read very widely in prose, but who will say quite callously, "No, I never read poetry." If the sales of modern poetry, distinctly labelled as such, were to cease entirely to-morrow not a publisher would fail; scarcely a publisher would be affected; and not a poet would die—for I do not believe that a single modern English poet is living to-day on the current proceeds of his verse. For a country which possesses the greatest poetical literature in the world this condition of affairs is at least odd. What makes it odder is that, occasionally, very occasionally, the average lettered man will have a fit of idolatry for a fine poet, buying his books in tens of thousands, and bestowing upon him immense riches. As with Tennyson. And what makes it odder still is that, after all, the average lettered man does not truly dislike poetry; he only dislikes it when it takes a certain form. He will read poetry and enjoy it, provided he is not aware that it is poetry. Poetry can exist authentically either in prose or in verse. Give him poetry concealed in prose and there is a chance that, taken off his guard, he will appreciate it. But show him a page of verse, and he will be ready to send for a policeman. The reason of this is that, though poetry may come to pass either in prose or in verse, it does actually happen far more frequently in verse than in prose; nearly all the very greatest poetry is in verse; verse is identified with the very greatest poetry, and the very greatest poetry can only be understood and savoured by people who have put themselves through a considerable mental discipline. To others it is an exasperating weariness. Hence chiefly the fearful prejudice of the average lettered man against the mere form of verse.

The formation of literary taste cannot be completed until that prejudice has been conquered. My very difficult task is to suggest a method of conquering it. I address myself exclusively to the large class of people who, if they are honest, will declare that, while they enjoy novels, essays, and history, they cannot "stand" verse. The case is extremely delicate, like all nervous cases. It is useless to employ the arts of reasoning, for the matter has got beyond logic; it is instinctive. Perfectly futile to assure you that verse will yield a higher percentage of pleasure than prose! You will reply: "We believe you, but that doesn't help us." Therefore I shall not argue. I shall venture to prescribe a curative treatment (doctors do not argue); and I beg you to follow it exactly, keeping your nerve and your calm. Loss of self-control might lead to panic, and panic would be fatal.

First: Forget as completely as you can all your present notions about the nature of verse and poetry. Take a sponge and wipe the slate of your mind. In particular, do not harass yourself by thoughts of metre and verse forms. Second: Read William Hazlitt's essay "On Poetry in General." This essay is the first in the book entitled *Lectures on the English Poets*. It can be bought in various forms. I think the cheapest satisfactory edition is in Routledge's "New Universal Library" (price 1s. net). I might have composed an essay of my own on the real harmless nature of poetry in general, but it could only have been an echo and a deterioration of Hazlitt's. He has put the truth about poetry in a way as interesting, clear, and reassuring as anyone is ever likely to put it. I do not expect, however, that you will instantly gather the full message and enthusiasm of the essay. It will probably seem to you not to "hang together." Still, it will leave bright bits of ideas in your mind. Third: After a week's interval read the essay again. On a second perusal it will appear more persuasive to you.

Fourth: Open the Bible and read the fortieth chapter of Isaiah. It is the chapter which begins, "Comfort ye, comfort ye, my people," and ends, "They shall run and not be weary, and they shall walk and not faint." This chapter will doubtless be more or less familiar to you. It cannot fail (whatever your particular *ism*) to impress you, to generate in your mind sensations which you recognise to be of a lofty and unusual order, and which you will admit to be pleasurable. You will probably agree that the result of reading this chapter (even if your particular *ism* is opposed to its authority) is finer than the result of reading a short story in a magazine or even an essay by Charles Lamb. Now the pleasurable sensations induced by the fortieth chapter of Isaiah are among the sensations usually induced by high-class poetry. The writer of it was a very great poet, and what he wrote is a very great poem. Fifth: After having read it, go back to Hazlitt, and see if you can find anything in Hazlitt's lecture which throws light on the psychology of your own emotions upon reading Isaiah.

Sixth: The next step is into unmistakable verse. It is to read one of Wordsworth's short narrative poems, *The Brothers*. There are editions of Wordsworth at a shilling, but I should advise the "Golden Treasury" Wordsworth (2s. 6d. net), because it contains the famous essay by Matthew Arnold, who made the selection. I want you to read this poem aloud. You will probably have to hide yourself somewhere in order to do so, for, of course, you would not, as yet, care to be overheard spouting poetry. Be good enough to forget that *The Brothers* is poetry. *The Brothers* is a short story, with a plain, clear plot. Read it as such. Read it simply for the story. It is very important at this critical stage that you should not embarrass your mind with preoccupations as to the *form* in which Wordsworth has told his story. Wordsworth's object was to tell a story as well as he could: just that. In reading aloud do not pay any more attention to the metre than you feel naturally inclined to pay. After a few lines the metre will present itself to you. Do not worry as to what kind of metre it is. When you have finished the perusal, examine your sensations . . .

Your sensations after reading this poem, and perhaps one or two other narrative poems of Wordsworth, such as *Michael*, will be different from the sensations produced in you by reading an ordinary, or even a very extraordinary, short story in prose. They may not be so sharp, so clear and piquant, but they will probably be, in their mysteriousness and their vagueness, more impressive. I do not say that they will be diverting. I do not go so far as to say that they will strike you as pleasing sensations. (Be it remembered that I am addressing myself to an imaginary tyro in poetry.) I would qualify them as being "disturbing." Well, to disturb the spirit is one of the greatest aims of art. And a disturbance of spirit is one of the finest pleasures that a highly-organised man can enjoy. But this truth can only be really learnt by the repetitions of experience. As an aid to the more exhaustive examination of your feelings under Wordsworth, in order that you may better understand what he was trying to effect in you, and the means which he employed, I must direct you to Wordsworth himself. Wordsworth, in addition to being a poet, was unsurpassed as a critic of poetry. What Hazlitt does for poetry in the way of creating enthusiasm Wordsworth does in the way of philosophic explanation. And Wordsworth's explanations of the theory and practice of poetry are written for the plain man. They pass the comprehension of nobody, and their direct, unassuming, and calm simplicity is extremely persuasive. Wordsworth's chief essays in throwing light on himself are the "Advertisement," "Preface," and "Appendix" to *Lyrical Ballads*; the letters to Lady Beaumont and "the Friend" and the "Preface" to the Poems dated 1815. All this matter is strangely interesting and of immense educational value. It is the first-class expert talking at ease about his subject. The essays relating to *Lyrical Ballads* will be the most useful for you. You will discover these precious documents in a volume entitled *Wordsworth's Literary Criticism* (published by Henry Frowde, 2s. 6d.), edited by that distinguished Wordsworthian Mr. Nowell C. Smith. It is essential that the student of poetry should become possessed, honestly or dishonestly, either of this volume or of the matter which it contains. There is, by the way, a volume of Wordsworth's prose in the Scott Library (1s.). Those who have not read Wordsworth on poetry can have no idea of the naïve charm and the helpful radiance of his expounding. I feel that I cannot too strongly press Wordsworth's criticism upon you.

Between Wordsworth and Hazlitt you will learn all that it behoves you to know of the nature, the aims, and the results of poetry. It is no part of my scheme to dot the "i's" and cross the "t's" of Wordsworth and Hazlitt. I best fulfil my purpose in urgently referring you to them. I have only a single point of my own to make—a psychological detail. One of the main obstacles to the cultivation of poetry in the average sensible man is an absurdly inflated notion of the ridiculous. At the bottom of that man's mind is the idea that poetry is "silly." He also finds it exaggerated and artificial; but these two accusations against poetry can be satisfactorily answered. The charge of silliness, of being ridiculous, however, cannot be refuted by argument. There is no logical answer to a guffaw. This sense of the ridiculous is merely a bad, infantile habit, in itself grotesquely ridiculous. You may see it particularly in the theatre. Not the greatest dramatist, not the greatest composer, not the greatest actor can prevent an audience from laughing uproariously at a tragic moment if a cat walks across the stage. But why ruin the scene by laughter? Simply because the majority of any audience is artistically childish. This sense of the ridiculous can only be crushed by the exercise of moral force. It can only be cowed. If you are inclined to laugh when a poet expresses himself more powerfully than you express yourself, when a poet talks about feelings which are not usually mentioned in daily papers, when a poet uses words and images which lie outside your vocabulary and range of thought, then you had better take yourself in hand. You have to decide whether you will be on the side of the angels or on the side of the nincompoops. There is no surer sign of imperfect development than the impulse to snigger at what is unusual, naïve, or exuberant. And if you choose to do so, you can detect the cat walking across the stage in the sublimest passages of literature. But more advanced souls will grieve for you.

The study of Wordsworth's criticism makes the seventh step in my course of treatment. The eighth is to return to those poems of Wordsworth's which you have already perused, and read them again in the full light of the author's defence and explanation. Read as much Wordsworth as you find you can assimilate, but do not attempt either of his long poems. The time, however, is now come for a long poem. I began by advising narrative poetry for the neophyte, and I shall persevere with the prescription. I mean narrative poetry in the restricted sense; for epic poetry is narrative. *Paradise Lost* is narrative; so is *The Prelude*. I suggest neither of these great works. My choice falls on Elizabeth Browning's *Aurora Leigh*. If you once work yourself "into" this poem, interesting yourself primarily (as with Wordsworth) in the events of the story, and not allowing yourself to be obsessed by the fact that what you are reading is "poetry"—if you do this, you are not likely to leave it unfinished. And before you reach the end you will have encountered *en route* pretty nearly all the moods of poetry that exist: tragic, humorous, ironic, elegiac, lyric—everything. You will have a comprehensive acquaintance with a poet's mind. I guarantee that you will come safely through if you treat the work as a novel. For a novel it effectively is, and a better one than any written by Charlotte Brontë or George Eliot. In reading, it would be well to mark, or take note of, the passages which give you the most pleasure, and then to compare these passages with the passages selected for praise by some authoritative critic. *Aurora Leigh* can be got in the "Temple Classics" (1s. 6d.), or in the "Canterbury Poets" (1s.). The indispensable biographical information about Mrs. Browning can be obtained from Mr. J.H. Ingram's short Life of her in the "Eminent Women" Series (1s. 6d.), or from *Robert Browning*, by William Sharp ("Great Writers" Series, 1s.).

This accomplished, you may begin to choose your poets. Going back to Hazlitt, you will see that he deals with, among others, Chaucer, Spenser, Shakespeare, Milton, Dryden, Pope, Chatterton, Burns, and the Lake School. You might select one of these, and read under his guidance. Said Wordsworth: "I was impressed by the conviction that there were four English poets whom I must have continually before me as examples—Chaucer, Shakespeare, Spenser, and Milton." (A word to the wise!) Wordsworth makes a fifth to these four. Concurrently with the careful, enthusiastic study of one of the undisputed classics, modern verse should be read. (I beg you to accept the following statement: that if the study of classical poetry inspires you with a distaste for modern poetry, then there is something seriously wrong in the method of your development.) You may at this stage (and not before) commence an inquiry into questions of rhythm, verse-structure, and rhyme. There is, I believe, no good, concise, cheap handbook to English prosody; yet such a manual is greatly needed. The only one with which I am acquainted is Tom Hood the younger's *Rules of Rhyme: A Guide to English Versification*. Again, the introduction to Walker's *Rhyming Dictionary* gives a fairly clear elementary account of the subject. Ruskin also has written an excellent essay on verse-rhythms. With a manual in front of you, you can acquire in a couple of hours a knowledge of the formal principles in which the music of English verse is rooted. The business is trifling. But the business of appreciating the inmost spirit of the greatest verse is tremendous and lifelong. It is not something that can be "got up."

CHAPTER X

BROAD COUNSELS

I have now set down what appear to me to be the necessary considerations, recommendations, exhortations, and dehortations in aid of this delicate and arduous enterprise of forming the literary taste. I have dealt with the theory of literature, with the psychology of the author, and—quite as important—with the psychology of the reader. I have tried to explain the author to the reader and the reader to himself. To go into further detail would be to exceed my original intention, with no hope of ever bringing the constantly-enlarging scheme to a logical conclusion. My aim is not to provide a map, but a compass—two very different instruments. In the way of general advice it remains for me only to put before you three counsels which apply more broadly than any I have yet offered to the business of reading.

You have within yourself a touchstone by which finally you can, and you must, test every book that your brain is capable of comprehending. Does the book seem to you to be sincere and true? If it does, then you need not worry about your immediate feelings, or the possible future consequences of the book. You will ultimately like the book, and you will be justified in liking it. Honesty, in literature as in life, is the quality that counts first and counts last. But beware of your immediate feelings. Truth is not always pleasant. The first glimpse of truth is, indeed, usually so disconcerting as to be positively unpleasant, and our impulse is to tell it to go away, for we will have no truck with it. If a book arouses your genuine contempt, you may dismiss it from your mind. Take heed, however, lest you confuse contempt with anger. If a book really moves you to anger, the chances are that it is a good book. Most good books have begun by causing anger which disguised itself as contempt. Demanding honesty from your authors, you must see that you render it yourself. And to be honest with oneself is not so simple as it appears. One's sensations and one's sentiments must be examined with detachment. When you have violently flung down a book, listen whether you can hear a faint voice saying within you: "It's true, though!" And if you catch the whisper, better yield to it as quickly as you can. For sooner or later the voice will win. Similarly, when you are hugging a book, keep your ear cocked for the secret warning: "Yes, but it isn't true." For bad books, by flattering you, by caressing, by appealing to the weak or the base in you, will often persuade you what fine and splendid books they are. (Of course, I use the word "true" in a wide and essential significance. I do not necessarily mean true to literal fact; I mean true to the plane of experience in which the book moves. The truthfulness of *Ivanhoe*, for example, cannot be estimated by the same standards as the truthfulness of Stubbs's *Constitutional History*.) In reading a book, a sincere questioning of oneself, "Is it true?" and a loyal abiding by the answer, will help more surely than any other process of ratiocination to form the taste. I will not assert that this question and answer are all-sufficient. A true book is not always great. But a great book is never untrue.

My second counsel is: In your reading you must have in view some definite aim—some aim other than the wish to derive pleasure. I conceive that to give pleasure is the highest end of any work of art, because the pleasure procured from any art is tonic, and transforms the life into which it enters. But the maximum of pleasure can only be obtained by regular effort, and regular effort implies the organisation of that effort. Open-air walking is a glorious exercise; it is the walking itself which is glorious. Nevertheless, when setting out for walking exercise, the sane man generally has a subsidiary aim in view. He says to himself either that he will reach a given point, or that he will progress at a given speed for a given distance, or that he will remain on his feet for a given time. He organises his effort, partly in order that he may combine some other advantage with the advantage of walking, but principally in order to be sure that the effort shall be an adequate effort. The same with reading. Your paramount aim in poring over literature is to enjoy, but you will not fully achieve that aim unless you have also a subsidiary aim which necessitates the measurement of your energy. Your subsidiary aim may be æsthetic, moral, political, religious, scientific, erudite; you may devote yourself to a man, a topic, an epoch, a nation, a branch of literature, an idea—you have the widest latitude in the choice of an objective; but a definite objective you must have. In my earlier remarks as to method in reading, I advocated, without insisting on, regular hours for study. But I both advocate and insist on the fixing of a date for the accomplishment of an allotted task. As an instance, it is not enough to say: "I will inform myself completely as to the Lake School." It is necessary to say: "I will inform myself completely as to the Lake School before I am a year older." Without this precautionary steeling of the resolution the risk of a humiliating collapse into futility is enormously magnified.

My third counsel is: Buy a library. It is obvious that you cannot read unless you have books. I began by urging the constant purchase of books— any books of approved quality, without reference to their immediate bearing upon your particular case. The moment has now come to inform you plainly that a bookman is, amongst other things, a man who possesses many books. A man who does not possess many books is not a bookman. For years literary authorities have been favouring the literary public with wondrously selected lists of "the best books"—the best novels, the best histories, the best poems, the best works of philosophy—or the hundred best or the fifty best of all sorts. The fatal disadvantage of such lists is that they leave out large quantities of literature which is admittedly first-class. The bookman cannot content himself with a selected library. He wants, as a minimum, a library reasonably complete in all departments.

With such a basis acquired, he can afterwards wander into those special byways of book-buying which happen to suit his special predilections. Every Englishman who is interested in any branch of his native literature, and who respects himself, ought to own a comprehensive and inclusive library of English literature, in comely and adequate editions. You may suppose that this counsel is a counsel of perfection. It is not. Mark Pattison laid down a rule that he who desired the name of book-lover must spend five per cent. of his income on books. The proposal does not seem extravagant, but even on a smaller percentage than five the average reader of these pages may become the owner, in a comparatively short space of time, of a reasonably complete English library, by which I mean a library containing the complete works of the supreme geniuses, representative important works of all the first-class men in all departments, and specimen works of all the men of the second rank whose reputation is really a living reputation to-day. The scheme for a library, which I now present, begins before Chaucer and ends with George Gissing, and I am fairly sure that the majority of people will be startled at the total inexpensiveness of it. So far as I am aware, no such scheme has ever been printed before.

CHAPTER XI

AN ENGLISH LIBRARY: PERIOD I

[For much counsel and correction in the matter of editions and prices I am indebted to my old and valued friend, Charles Young, head of the firm of Lamley & Co., booksellers, South Kensington.]

For the purposes of book-buying, I divide English literature, not strictly into historical epochs, but into three periods which, while scarcely arbitrary from the historical point of view, have nevertheless been calculated according to the space which they will occupy on the shelves and to the demands which they will make on the purse:

I.   From the beginning to John Dryden, or roughly, to the end of the seventeenth century.
II. From William Congreve to Jane Austen, or roughly, the eighteenth century.
III. From Sir Walter Scott to the last deceased author who is recognised as a classic, or roughly, the nineteenth century.

Period III. will bulk the largest and cost the most; not necessarily because it contains more absolutely great books than the other periods (though in my opinion it *does*), but because it is nearest to us, and therefore fullest of interest for us.

I have not confined my choice to books of purely literary interest—that is to say, to works which are primarily works of literary art. Literature is the vehicle of philosophy, science, morals, religion, and history; and a library which aspires to be complete must comprise, in addition to imaginative works, all these branches of intellectual activity. Comprising all these branches, it cannot avoid comprising works of which the purely literary interest is almost nil.

On the other hand, I have excluded from consideration:—

i. Works whose sole importance is that they form a link in the chain of development. For example, nearly all the productions of authors between Chaucer and the beginning of the Elizabethan period, such as Gower, Hoccleve, and Skelton, whose works, for sufficient reason, are read only by professors and students who mean to be professors.

ii. Works not originally written in English, such as the works of that very great philosopher Roger Bacon, of whom this isle ought to be prouder than it is. To this rule, however, I have been constrained to make a few exceptions. Sir Thomas More's *Utopia* was written in Latin, but one does not easily conceive a library to be complete without it. And could one exclude Sir Isaac Newton's *Principia*, the masterpiece of the greatest physicist that the world has ever seen? The law of gravity ought to have, and does have, a powerful sentimental interest for us.

iii. Translations from foreign literature into English.

Here, then, are the lists for the first period:

PROSE WRITERS.

	£	s.	d.
Bede, *Ecclesiastical History*: Temple Classics	0	1	6
Sir Thomas Malory, *Morte d'Arthur*: Everyman's Library (4 vols.).	0	4	0

120

Sir Thomas More, *Utopia*: Scott Library	0	1	0
George Cavendish, *Life of Cardinal Wolsey*: New Universal Library.	0	1	0
Richard Hakluyt, *Voyages*: Everyman's Library (8 vols.).	0	8	0
Richard Hooker, *Ecclesiastical Polity*: Everyman's Library (2 vols.).	0	2	0
Francis Bacon, *Works*: Newnes's Thinpaper Classics.	0	2	0
Thomas Dekker, *Gull's Horn-Book*: King's Classics.	0	1	6
Lord Herbert of Cherbury, *Autobiography*: Scott Library.	0	1	0
John Selden, *Table-Talk*: New Universal Library.	0	1	0
Thomas Hobbes, *Leviathan*: New Universal Library.	0	1	0
James Howell, *Familiar Letters*: Temple Classics (3 vols.).	0	4	6
Sir Thomas Browne, *Religio Medici*, etc.: Everyman's Library.	0	1	0
Jeremy Taylor, *Holy Living and Holy Dying*: Temple Classics (3 vols.).	0	4	6
Izaak Walton, *Compleat Angler*: Everyman's Library.	0	1	0
John Bunyan, *Pilgrim's Progress*: World's Classics.	0	1	0
Sir William Temple, *Essay on Gardens of Epicurus*: King's Classics.	0	1	6
John Evelyn, *Diary*: Everyman's Library (2 vols.).	0	2	0
Samuel Pepys, *Diary*: Everyman's Library (2 vols.).	0	2	0
	£2	1	6

The principal omission from the above list is *The Paston Letters*, which I should probably have included had the enterprise of publishers been sufficient to put an edition on the market at a cheap price. Other omissions include the works of Caxton and Wyclif, and such books as Camden's

Britannia, Ascham's *Schoolmaster*, and Fuller's *Worthies*, whose lack of first-rate value as literature is not adequately compensated by their historical interest. As to the Bible, in the first place it is a translation, and in the second I assume that you already possess a copy.

POETS.

	£	s.	d.
Beowulf, Routledge's London Library	0	2	6
GEOFFREY CHAUCER, Works: Globe Edition	0	3	6
Nicolas Udall, Ralph Roister-Doister: Temple Dramatists	0	1	0
EDMUND SPENSER, Works: Globe Edition	0	3	6
Thomas Lodge, Rosalynde: Caxton Series	0	1	0
Robert Greene, Tragical Reign of Selimus: Temple Dramatists	0	1	0
Michael Drayton, Poems: Newnes's Pocket Classics	0	8	6
CHRISTOPHER MARLOWE, Works: New Universal Library	0	1	0
WILLIAM SHAKESPEARE, Works: Globe Edition	0	3	6
Thomas Campion, Poems: Muses' Library	0	1	0
Ben Jonson, Plays: Canterbury Poets	0	1	0
John Donne, Poems: Muses' Library (2 vols.)	0	2	0
John Webster, Cyril Tourneur, Plays: Mermaid Series	0	2	6
Philip Massinger, Plays: Cunningham Edition	0	3	6
Beaumont and Fletcher, Plays: a Selection Canterbury Poets	0	1	0
John Ford, Plays: Mermaid Series	0	2	6
George Herbert, The Temple: Everyman's Library	0	1	0
ROBERT HERRICK, Poems: Muses' Library (2 vols.)	0	2	0

Edmund Waller, Poems: Muses' Library (2 vols.)	0	2	0
Sir John Suckling, Poems: Muses' Library	0	1	0
Abraham Cowley, English Poems: Cambridge University Press	0	4	6
Richard Crashaw, Poems: Muses' Library	0	1	0
Henry Vaughan, Poems: Methuen's Little Library	0	1	6
Samuel Butler, Hudibras: Cambridge University Press	0	4	6
JOHN MILTON, Poetical Works: Oxford Cheap Edition	0	2	0
JOHN MILTON, Select Prose Works: Scott Library	0	1	0
Andrew Marvell, Poems: Methuen's Little Library	0	1	6
John Dryden, Poetical Works: Globe Edition	0	3	6
[Thomas Percy], Reliques of Ancient English Poetry: Everyman's Library (2 vols.)	0	2	0
Arber's "Spenser" Anthology: Oxford University Press	0	2	0
Arber's "Jonson" Anthology: Oxford University Press	0	2	0
Arber's "Shakspere" Anthology: Oxford University Press	0	2	0
	———	———	——
	£3	7	6

There were a number of brilliant minor writers in the seventeenth century whose best work, often trifling in bulk, either scarcely merits the acquisition of a separate volume for each author, or cannot be obtained at all in a modern edition. Such authors, however, may not be utterly neglected in the formation of a library. It is to meet this difficulty that I have included the last three volumes on the above list. Professor Arber's anthologies are full of rare pieces, and comprise admirable specimens of the verse of Samuel Daniel, Giles Fletcher, Countess of Pembroke,

James I., George Peele, Sir Walter Raleigh, Thomas Sackville, Sir Philip Sidney, Drummond of Hawthornden, Thomas Heywood, George Wither, Sir Henry Wotton, Sir William Davenant, Thomas Randolph, Frances Quarles, James Shirley, and other greater and lesser poets.

I have included all the important Elizabethan dramatists except John Marston, all the editions of whose works, according to my researches, are out of print.

In the Elizabethan and Jacobean periods talent was so extraordinarily plentiful that the standard of excellence is quite properly raised, and certain authors are thus relegated to the third, or excluded, class who in a less fertile period would have counted as at least second-class.

SUMMARY OF THE FIRST PERIOD.

			£	s.	d.
19 prose authors in	36 volumes	costing	2	1	6
29 poets in	36 "	"	3	7	6
48	72		£5	9	0

In addition, scores of authors of genuine interest are represented in the anthologies.

The prices given are gross, and in many instances there is a 25 per cent. discount to come off. All the volumes can be procured immediately at any bookseller's.

CHAPTER XII

AN ENGLISH LIBRARY: PERIOD II

After dealing with the formation of a library of authors up to John Dryden, I must logically arrange next a scheme for the period covered roughly by the eighteenth century. There is, however, no reason why the student in quest of a library should follow the chronological order. Indeed, I should advise him to attack the nineteenth century before the eighteenth, for the reason that, unless his taste happens to be peculiarly "Augustan," he will obtain a more immediate satisfaction and profit from his acquisitions in the nineteenth century than in the eighteenth. There is in eighteenth-century literature a considerable proportion of what I may term "unattractive excellence," which one must have for the purposes of completeness, but which may await actual perusal until more pressing and more human books have been read. I have particularly in mind the philosophical authors of the century.

PROSE WRITERS.

	£	s.	d.
JOHN LOCKE, *Philosophical Works*: Bohn's Edition (2 vols.)	0	7	0
SIR ISAAC NEWTON, *Principia* (sections 1, 2, and 3): Macmillans	0	12	0
Gilbert Burnet, *History of His Own Time*: Everyman's Library	0	1	0

William Wycherley, *Best Plays*: Mermaid Series	0	2	6
WILLIAM CONGREVE, *Best Plays*: Mermaid Series	0	2	6
Jonathan Swift, *Tale of a Tub*: Scott Library	0	1	0
Jonathan Swift, *Gulliver's Travels*: Temple Classics	0	1	6
DANIEL DEFOE, *Robinson Crusoe*: World's Classics	0	1	0
DANIEL DEFOE, *Journal of the Plague Year*: Everyman's Library	0	1	0
Joseph Addison, Sir Richard Steele, *Essays*: Scott Library	0	1	0
William Law, *Serious Call*: Everyman's Library	0	1	0
Lady Mary W. Montagu, *Letters*: Everyman's Library	0	1	0
George Berkeley, *Principles of Human Knowledge*: New Universal Library	0	1	0
SAMUEL RICHARDSON, *Clarissa* (abridged): Routledge's Edition	0	2	0
John Wesley, *Journal*: Everyman's Library (4 vols.)	0	4	0
HENRY FIELDING, *Tom Jones*: Routledge's Edition	0	2	0
HENRY FIELDING, *Amelia*: Routledge's Edition	0	2	0
HENRY FIELDING, *Joseph Andrews*: Routledge's Edition	0	2	0
David Hume, *Essays*: World's Classics	0	1	0
LAURENCE STERNE, *Tristram Shandy*: World's Classics	0	1	0
LAURENCE STERNE, *Sentimental Journey*: New Universal Library	0	1	0
Horace Walpole, *Castle of Otranto*: King's Classics	0	1	6
Tobias Smollett, *Humphrey Clinker*: Routledge's Edition	0	2	0
Tobias Smollett, *Travels through France*			

and Italy: World's Classics	0	1	0
ADAM SMITH, *Wealth of Nations*: World's Classics (2 vols.)	0	2	0
Samuel Johnson, *Lives of the Poets*: World's Classics (2 vols.)	0	2	0
Samuel Johnson, *Rasselas*: New Universal Library	0	1	0
JAMES BOSWELL, *Life of Johnson*: Everyman's Library (2 vols.)	0	2	0
Oliver Goldsmith, *Works*: Globe Edition	0	3	6
Henry Mackenzie, *The Man of Feeling*: Cassell's National Library	0	0	6
Sir Joshua Reynolds, *Discourses on Art*: Scott Library	0	1	0
Edmund Burke, *Reflections on the French Revolution*: Scott Library	0	1	0
Edmund Burke, *Thoughts on the Present Discontents*: New Universal Library	0	1	0
EDWARD GIBBON, *Decline and Fall of the Roman Empire*: World's Classics (7 vols.)	0	7	0
Thomas Paine, *Rights of Man*: Watts and Co.'s Edition	0	1	0
RICHARD BRINSLEY SHERIDAN, *Plays*: World's Classics	0	1	0
Fanny Burney, *Evelina*: Everyman's Library	0	1	0
Gilbert White, *Natural History of Selborne*: Everyman's Library	0	1	0
Arthur Young, *Travels in France*: York Library	0	2	0
Mungo Park, *Travels*: Everyman's Library	0	1	0
Jeremy Bentham, *Introduction to the Principles of Morals*: Clarendon Press	0	6	6
THOMAS ROBERT MALTHUS, *Essay on the Principle of Population*: Ward, Lock's Edition	0	3	0
William Godwin, *Caleb Williams*: Newnes's Edition	0	1	0

	£	s.	d.
Maria Edgeworth, *Helen*: Macmillan's Illustrated Edition	0	2	6
JANE AUSTEN, *Novels*: Nelson's New Century Library (2 vols.)	0	4	0
James Morier, *Hadji Baba*: Macmillan's Illustrated Novels	0	2	6
	£5	1	0

The principal omissions here are Jeremy Collier, whose outcry against the immorality of the stage is his slender title to remembrance; Richard Bentley, whose scholarship principally died with him, and whose chief works are no longer current; and "Junius," who would have been deservedly forgotten long ago had there been a contemporaneous Sherlock Holmes to ferret out his identity.

POETS.

	£	s.	d.
Thomas Otway, *Venice Preserved*: Temple Dramatists	0	1	0
Matthew Prior, *Poems on Several Occasions*: Cambridge English Classics	0	4	6
John Gay, *Poems*: Muses' Library (2 vols.)	0	2	0
ALEXANDER POPE, *Works*: Globe Edition	0	3	0
Isaac Watts, *Hymns*: Any hymn-book	0	1	0
James Thomson, *The Seasons*: Muses' Library	0	1	0
Charles Wesley, *Hymns*: Any hymn-book	0	1	0
THOMAS GRAY, Samuel Johnson, William Collins, *Poems*: Muses' Library	0	1	0
James Macpherson (Ossian), *Poems*: Canterbury Poets	0	1	0
THOMAS CHATTERTON, *Poems*: Muses' Library (2 vols.)	0	2	0

WILLIAM COWPER, *Poems*: Canterbury Poets	0	1	0
WILLIAM COWPER, *Letters*: World's Classics	0	1	0
George Crabbe, *Poems*: Methuen's Little Library	0	1	6
WILLIAM BLAKE, *Poems*: Muses' Library	0	1	0
William Lisle Bowles, Hartley Coleridge, *Poems*: Canterbury Poets	0	1	0
ROBERT BURNS, *Works*: Globe Edition	0	3	6
	£1	7	0

SUMMARY OF THE PERIOD.

39 prose writers in	60	volumes,	costing	£5	1	0
18 poets	18	"	"	1	7	0
57	78			£6	8	0

CHAPTER XIII

AN ENGLISH LIBRARY: PERIOD III

The catalogue of necessary authors of this third and last period being so long, it is convenient to divide the prose writers into Imaginative and Non-imaginative.

In the latter half of the period the question of copyright affects our scheme to a certain extent, because it affects prices. Fortunately it is the fact that no single book of recognised first-rate general importance is conspicuously dear. Nevertheless, I have encountered difficulties in the second rank; I have dealt with them in a spirit of compromise. I think I may say that, though I should have included a few more authors had their books been obtainable at a reasonable price, I have omitted none that I consider indispensable to a thoroughly representative collection. No living author is included.

Where I do not specify the edition of a book the original copyright edition is meant.

PROSE WRITERS: IMAGINATIVE.

	£	s.	d.
SIR WALTER SCOTT, *Waverley, Heart of Midlothian, Quentin Durward, Red-gauntlet, Ivanhoe*: Everyman's Library (5 vols.)	0	5	0
SIR WALTER SCOTT, *Marmion*, etc.: Canterbury Poets	0	1	0
Charles Lamb, *Works in Prose and Verse*:			

Clarendon Press (2 vols.)	0	4	0
Charles Lamb, *Letters*: Newnes's Thin			
Paper Classics	0	2	0
Walter Savage Landor, *Imaginary Conversations*:			
Scott Library	0	1	0
Walter Savage Landor, *Poems*: Canterbury			
Poets	0	1	0
Leigh Hunt, *Essays and Sketches*: World's			
Classics	0	1	0
Thomas Love Peacock, *Principal Novels*:			
New Universal Library (2 vols.)	0	2	0
Mary Russell Mitford, *Our Village*:			
Scott Library	0	1	0
Michael Scott, *Tom Cringle's Log*: Macmillan's			
Illustrated Novels	0	2	6
Frederick Marryat, *Mr. Midshipman*			
Easy: Everyman's Library	0	1	0
John Galt, *Annals of the Parish*: Everyman's			
Library	0	1	0
Susan Ferrier, *Marriage*: Routledge's			
edition	0	2	0
Douglas Jerrold, *Mrs. Caudle's Curtain*			
Lectures: World's Classics	0	1	0
Lord Lytton, *Last Days of Pompeii*:			
Everyman's Library	0	1	0
William Carleton, *Stories*: Scott Library	0	1	0
Charles James Lever, *Harry Lorrequer*:			
Everyman's Library	0	1	0
Harrison Ainsworth, *The Tower of London*:			
New Universal Library	0	1	0
George Henry Borrow, *Bible in Spain*,			
Lavengro: New Universal Library (2 vols.)	0	2	0
Lord Beaconsfield, *Sybil, Coningsby*:			
Lane's New Pocket Library (2 vols.)	0	2	0
W.M. THACKERAY, *Vanity Fair, Esmond*:			
Everyman's Library (2 vols.)	0	2	0
W.M. THACKERAY, *Barry Lyndon*, and			
Roundabout Papers, etc.:			
Nelson's New Century Library	0	2	0
CHARLES DICKENS, *Works*: Everyman's			

Library (18 vols.)	0	18	0
Charles Reade, *The Cloister and the Hearth*: Everyman's Library	0	1	0
Anthony Trollope, *Barchester Towers, Framley Parsonage*: Lane's New Pocket Library (2 vols.)	0	2	0
Charles Kingsley, *Westward Ho!*: Everyman's Library	0	1	0
Henry Kingsley, *Ravenshoe*: Everyman's Library	0	1	0
Charlotte Brontë, *Jane Eyre, Shirley, Villette, Professor, and Poems*: World's Classics (4 vols.)	0	4	0
Emily Brontë, *Wuthering Heights*: World's Classics	0	1	0
Elizabeth Gaskell, *Cranford*: World's Classics	0	1	0
Elizabeth Gaskell, *Life of Charlotte Brontë*	0	2	6
George Eliot, *Adam Bede, Silas Marner, The Mill on the Floss*: Everyman's Library (3 vols.)	0	3	0
G.J. Whyte-Melville, *The Gladiators*: New Universal Library	0	1	0
Alexander Smith, *Dreamthorpe*: New Universal Library	0	1	0
George Macdonald, *Malcolm*	0	1	6
Walter Pater, *Imaginary Portraits*	0	6	0
Wilkie Collins, *The Woman in White*	0	1	0
R.D. Blackmore, *Lorna Doone*: Everyman's Library	0	1	0
Samuel Butler, *Erewhon*: Fifield's Edition	0	2	6
Laurence Oliphant, *Altiora Peto*	0	3	6
Margaret Oliphant, *Salem Chapel*: Everyman's Library	0	1	0
Richard Jefferies, *Story of My Heart*	0	2	0
Lewis Carroll, *Alice in Wonderland*: Macmillan's Cheap Edition	0	1	0
John Henry Shorthouse, *John Inglesant*: Macmillan's Pocket Classics	0	2	0

	£	s.	d.
R.L. Stevenson, *Master of Ballantrae, Virginibus Puerisque*: Pocket Edition (2 vols.)	0	4	0
George Gissing, *The Odd Women*: Popular Edition (bound)	0	0	7
	£5	0	1

Names such as those of Charlotte Yonge and Dinah Craik are omitted intentionally.

PROSE WRITERS: NON-IMAGINATIVE.

	£	s.	d.
William Hazlitt, *Spirit of the Age*: World's Classics	0	1	0
William Hazlitt, *English Poets and Comic Writers*: Bohn's Library	0	3	6
Francis Jeffrey, *Essays from Edinburgh Review*: New Universal Library	0	1	0
Thomas de Quincey, *Confessions of an English Opium-eater*, etc.: Scott Library	0	1	0
Sydney Smith, *Selected Papers*: Scott Library	0	1	0
George Finlay, *Byzantine Empire*: Everyman's Library	0	1	0
John G. Lockhart, *Life of Scott*: Everyman's Library	0	1	0
Agnes Strickland, *Life of Queen Elizabeth*: Everyman's Library	0	1	0
Hugh Miller, *Old Red Sandstone*: Everyman's Library	0	1	0
J.H. Newman, *Apologia pro vita sua*: New Universal Library	0	1	0
Lord Macaulay, *History of England*, (3), *Essays* (2): Everyman's Library (5 vols.)	0	5	0
A.P. Stanley, *Memorials of Canterbury*:			

Everyman's Library	0	1	0
THOMAS CARLYLE, *French Revolution* (2), *Cromwell* (3), *Sartor Resartus and Heroes and Hero-Worship* (1): Everyman's Library (6 vols.)	0	6	0
THOMAS CARLYLE, *Latter-day Pamphlets*: Chapman and Hall's Edition	0	1	0
CHARLES DARWIN, *Origin of Species*: Murray's Edition	0	1	0
CHARLES DARWIN, *Voyage of the Beagle*: Everyman's Library	0	1	0
A.W. Kinglake, *Eothen*: New Universal Library	0	1	0
John Stuart Mill, *Auguste Comte and Positivism*: New Universal Library	0	1	0
John Brown, *Horæ Subsecivæ*: World's Classics	0	1	0
John Brown, *Rab and His Friends*: Everyman's Library	0	1	0
Sir Arthur Helps, *Friends in Council*: New Universal Library	0	1	0
Mark Pattison, *Life of Milton*: English Men of Letters Series	0	1	0
F.W. Robertson, *On Religion and Life*: Everyman's Library	0	1	0
Benjamin Jowett, *Interpretation of Scripture*: Routledge's London Library	0	2	6
George Henry Lewes, *Principles of Success in Literature*: Scott Library	0	1	0
Alexander Bain, *Mind and Body*	0	4	0
James Anthony Froude, *Dissolution of the Monasteries*, etc.: New Universal Library	0	1	0
Mary Wollstonecraft, *Vindication of the Rights of Women*: Scott Library	0	1	0
John Tyndall, *Glaciers of the Alps*: Everyman's Library	0	1	0
Sir Henry Maine, *Ancient Law*: New Universal Library	0	1	0
JOHN RUSKIN, *Seven Lamps* (1), *Sesame*			

and Lilies (1), *Stones of Venice* (3):			
George Allen's Cheap Edition (5 vols.)	0	5	0
HERBERT SPENCER, *First Principles* (2 vols.)	0	2	0
HERBERT SPENCER, *Education*	0	1	0
Sir Richard Burton, *Narrative of a Pilgrimage to Mecca*: Bohn's Edition (2 vols.)	0	7	0
J.S. Speke, *Sources of the Nile*: Everyman's Library	0	1	0
Thomas Henry Huxley, *Essays*: Everyman's Library	0	1	0
E.A. Freeman, *Europe*: Macmillan's Primers	0	1	0
WILLIAM STUBBS, *Early Plantagenets*	0	2	0
Walter Bagehot, *Lombard Street*	0	3	6
Richard Holt Hutton, *Cardinal Newman*	0	3	6
Sir John Seeley, *Ecce Homo*: New Universal Library	0	1	0
David Masson, *Thomas de Quincey*: English Men of Letters Series	0	1	0
John Richard Green, *Short History of the English People*	0	8	6
Sir Leslie Stephen, *Pope*: English Men of Letters Series	0	1	0
Lord Acton, *On the Study of History*	0	2	6
Mandell Creighton, *The Age of Elizabeth*	0	2	6
F.W.H. Myers, *Wordsworth*: English Men of Letters Series	0	1	0
	£4	10	6

The following authors are omitted, I think justifiably:—Hallam, Whewell, Grote, Faraday, Herschell, Hamilton, John Wilson, Richard Owen, Stirling Maxwell, Buckle, Oscar Wilde, P.G. Hamerton, F.D. Maurice, Henry Sidgwick, and Richard Jebb.

Lastly, here is the list of poets. In the matter of price per volume it is the most expensive of all the lists. This is due to the fact that it contains a larger proportion of copyright works. Where I do not specify the edition of a book, the original copyright edition is meant:

POETS.

	£	s.	d.
WILLIAM WORDSWORTH, *Poetical Works*: Oxford Edition	0	3	6
WILLIAM WORDSWORTH, *Literary Criticism*: Nowell Smith's Edition	0	2	6
Robert Southey, *Poems*: Canterbury Poets	0	1	0
Robert Southey, *Life of Nelson*: Everyman's Library	0	1	0
S.T. COLERIDGE, *Poetical Works*: Newnes's Thin Paper Classics	0	2	0
S.T. COLERIDGE, *Biographia Literaria*: Everyman's Library	0	1	0
S.T. COLERIDGE, *Lectures on Shakspere*: Everyman's Library	0	1	0
JOHN KEATS, *Poetical Works*: Oxford Edition	0	3	6
PERCY BYSSHE SHELLEY, *Poetical Works*: Oxford Edition	0	3	6
LORD BYRON, *Poems*: E. Hartley Coleridge's Edition	0	6	0
LORD BYRON, *Letters*: Scott Library	0	1	0
Thomas Hood, *Poems*: World's Classics	0	1	0
James and Horace Smith, *Rejected Addresses*: New Universal Library	0	1	0
John Keble, *The Christian Year*: Canterbury Poets	0	1	0
George Darley, *Poems*: Muses' Library	0	1	0
T.L. Beddoes, *Poems*: Muses' Library	0	1	0
Thomas Moore, *Selected Poems*: Canterbury Poets	0	1	0
James Clarence Mangan, *Poems*: D.J. O'Donoghue's Edition	0	3	6
W. Mackworth Praed, *Poems*: Canterbury			

	£	s	d
Poets	0	1	0
R.S. Hawker, *Cornish Ballads*: C.E. Byles's Edition	0	5	0
Edward FitzGerald, *Omar Khayyam*: Golden Treasury Series	0	2	6
P.J. Bailey, *Festus*: Routledge's Edition	0	3	6
Arthur Hugh Clough, *Poems*: Muses' Library	0	1	0
LORD TENNYSON, *Poetical Works*: Globe Edition	0	3	6
ROBERT BROWNING, *Poetical Works*: World's Classics (2 vols.)	0	2	0
Elizabeth Browning, *Aurora Leigh*: Temple Classics	0	1	6
Elizabeth Browning, *Shorter Poems*: Canterbury Poets	0	1	0
P.B. Marston, *Song-tide*: Canterbury Poets	0	1	0
Aubrey de Vere, *Legends of St. Patrick*: Cassell's National Library	0	0	6
MATTHEW ARNOLD, *Poems*: Golden Treasury Series	0	2	6
MATTHEW ARNOLD, *Essays*: Everyman's Library	0	1	0
Coventry Patmore, *Poems*: Muses' Library	0	1	0
Sydney Dobell, *Poems*: Canterbury Poets	0	1	0
Eric Mackay, *Love-letters of a Violinist*: Canterbury Poets	0	1	0
T.E. Brown, *Poems*	0	7	6
C.S. Calverley, *Verses and Translations*	0	1	6
D.G. ROSSETTI, *Poetical Works*	0	3	6
Christina Rossetti, *Selected Poems*: Golden Treasury Series	0	2	6
James Thomson, *City of Dreadful Night*	0	3	6
Jean Ingelow, *Poems*: Red Letter Library	0	1	6
William Morris, *The Earthly Paradise*	0	6	0
William Morris, *Early Romances*: Everyman's Library	0	1	0
Augusta Webster, *Selected Poems*	0	4	6

W.E. Henley, *Poetical Works*	0	6	0
Francis Thompson, *Selected Poems*	0	5	0
	£5	7	0

Poets whom I have omitted after hesitation are: Ebenezer Elliott, Thomas Woolner, William Barnes, Gerald Massey, and Charles Jeremiah Wells. On the other hand, I have had no hesitation about omitting David Moir, Felicia Hemans, Aytoun, Sir Edwin Arnold, and Sir Lewis Morris. I have included John Keble in deference to much enlightened opinion, but against my inclination. There are two names in the list which may be somewhat unfamiliar to many readers. James Clarence Mangan is the author of *My Dark Rosaleen*, an acknowledged masterpiece, which every library must contain. T.E. Brown is a great poet, recognised as such by a few hundred people, and assuredly destined to a far wider fame. I have included FitzGerald because *Omar Khayyam* is much less a translation than an original work.

SUMMARY OF THE NINETEENTH CENTURY.

83 prose-writers, in	141	volumes, costing	£9	10	7
38 poets	46	""	5	7	0
121	187		£14	17	7

GRAND SUMMARY OF COMPLETE LIBRARY.

	Authors.	Volumes.	Price.		
1. To Dryden	48	72	£5	9	0
2. Eighteenth Century	57	78	6	8	0
3. Nineteenth Century	121	187	14	17	7
	226	337	£26	14	7

I think it will be agreed that the total cost of this library is surprisingly small. By laying out the sum of sixpence a day for three years you may become the possessor of a collection of books which, for range and completeness in all branches of literature, will bear comparison with libraries far more imposing, more numerous, and more expensive.

I have mentioned the question of discount. The discount which you will obtain (even from a bookseller in a small town) will be more than sufficient to pay for Chambers's *Cyclopædia of English Literature*, three volumes, price 30s. net. This work is indispensable to a bookman. Personally, I owe it much.

When you have read, wholly or in part, a majority of these three hundred and thirty-five volumes, *with enjoyment*, you may begin to whisper to yourself that your literary taste is formed; and you may pronounce judgment on modern works which come before the bar of your opinion in the calm assurance that, though to err is human, you do at any rate know what you are talking about.

CHAPTER XIV

MENTAL STOCKTAKING

Great books do not spring from something accidental in the great men who wrote them. They are the effluence of their very core, the expression of the life itself of the authors. And literature cannot be said to have served its true purpose until it has been translated into the actual life of him who reads. It does not succeed until it becomes the vehicle of the vital. Progress is the gradual result of the unending battle between human reason and human instinct, in which the former slowly but surely wins. The most powerful engine in this battle is literature. It is the vast reservoir of true ideas and high emotions—and life is constituted of ideas and emotions. In a world deprived of literature, the intellectual and emotional activity of all but a few exceptionally gifted men would quickly sink and retract to a narrow circle. The broad, the noble, the generous would tend to disappear for want of accessible storage. And life would be correspondingly degraded, because the fallacious idea and the petty emotion would never feel the upward pull of the ideas and emotions of genius. Only by conceiving a society without literature can it be clearly realised that the function of literature is to raise the plain towards the top level of the peaks. Literature exists so that where one man has lived finely ten thousand may afterwards live finely. It is a means of life; it concerns the living essence.

Of course, literature has a minor function, that of passing the time in an agreeable and harmless fashion, by giving momentary faint pleasure. Vast multitudes of people (among whom may be numbered not a few habitual readers) utilise only this minor function of literature; by implication they class it with golf, bridge, or soporifics. Literary genius, however, had no intention of competing with these devices for fleeting the empty hours; and all such use of literature may be left out of account.

You, O serious student of many volumes, believe that you have a sincere passion for reading. You hold literature in honour, and your last wish would be to debase it to a paltry end. You are not of those who read because the clock has just struck nine and one can't go to bed till eleven. You are animated by a real desire to get out of literature all that literature will give. And in that aim you keep on reading, year after year, and the grey hairs come. But amid all this steady tapping of the reservoir, do you ever take stock of what you have acquired? Do you ever pause to make a valuation, in terms of your own life, of that which you are daily absorbing, or imagine you are absorbing? Do you ever satisfy yourself by proof that you are absorbing anything at all, that the living waters, instead of vitalising you, are not running off you as though you were a duck in a storm? Because, if you omit this mere business precaution, it may well be that you, too, without knowing it, are little by little joining the triflers who read only because eternity is so long. It may well be that even your alleged sacred passion is, after all, simply a sort of drug-habit. The suggestion disturbs and worries you. You dismiss it impatiently; but it returns.

How (you ask, unwillingly) can a man perform a mental stocktaking? How can he put a value on what he gets from books? How can he effectively test, in cold blood, whether he is receiving from literature all that literature has to give him?

The test is not so vague, nor so difficult, as might appear.

If a man is not thrilled by intimate contact with nature: with the sun, with the earth, which is his origin and the arouser of his acutest emotions—

If he is not troubled by the sight of beauty in many forms—

If he is devoid of curiosity concerning his fellow-men and his fellow-animals—

If he does not have glimpses of the nuity of all things in an orderly progress—

If he is chronically "querulous, dejected, and envious"—

If he is pessimistic—

If he is of those who talk about "this age of shams," "this age without ideals," "this hysterical age," and this heaven-knows-what-age—

Then that man, though he reads undisputed classics for twenty hours a day, though he has a memory of steel, though he rivals Porson in scholarship and Sainte Beuve in judgment, is not receiving from literature what literature has to give. Indeed, he is chiefly wasting his time. Unless he can read differently, it were better for him if he sold all his books, gave to the poor, and played croquet. He fails because he has not assimilated into his existence the vital essences which genius put into the books that have merely passed before his eyes; because genius has offered him faith, courage, vision, noble passion, curiosity, love, a thirst for beauty, and he has not taken the gift; because genius has offered him the chance of living fully, and he is only half alive, for it is only in the stress of fine ideas and emotions that a man may be truly said to live. This is not a moral invention, but a simple fact, which will be attested by all who know what that stress is.

What! You talk learnedly about Shakespeare's sonnets! Have you heard Shakespeare's terrific shout:

> Full many a glorious morning have I seen
> > Flatter the mountain-tops with sovereign eye,
> Kissing with golden face the meadows green,
> > Gilding pale streams with heavenly alchemy.

And yet, can you see the sun over the viaduct at Loughborough Junction of a morning, and catch its rays in the Thames off Dewar's whisky monument, and not shake with the joy of life? If so, you and

Shakespeare are not yet in communication. What! You pride yourself on your beautiful edition of Casaubon's translation of *Marcus Aurelius*, and you savour the cadences of the famous:

> This day I shall have to do with an idle, curious man, with an unthankful man, a railer, a crafty, false, or an envious man. All these ill qualities have happened unto him, through ignorance of that which is truly good and truly bad. But I that understand the nature of that which is good, that it only is to be desired, and of that which is bad, that it only is truly odious and shameful: who know, moreover, that this transgressor, whosoever he be, is my kinsman, not by the same blood and seed, but by participation of the same reason and of the same divine particle—how can I be hurt? . . .

And with these cadences in your ears you go and quarrel with a cabman!

You would be ashamed of your literary self to be caught in ignorance of Whitman, who wrote:

Now understand me well—it is provided in the essence of things that from any fruition of success, no matter what, shall come forth something to make a greater struggle necessary.

And yet, having achieved a motor-car, you lose your temper when it breaks down half-way up a hill!

You know your Wordsworth, who has been trying to teach you about:

> The Upholder of the tranquil soul
> That tolerates the indignities of Time
> And, from the centre of Eternity
> All finite motions over-ruling, lives
> In glory immutable.

But you are capable of being seriously unhappy when your suburban train selects a tunnel for its repose!

And the A.V. of the Bible, which you now read, not as your forefathers read it, but with an æsthetic delight, especially in the Apocrypha! You remember:

> Whatsoever is brought upon thee, take cheerfully, and be patient when thou art changed to a low estate. For gold is tried in the fire and acceptable men in the furnace of adversity.

And yet you are ready to lie down and die because a woman has scorned you! Go to!

You think some of my instances approach the ludicrous? They do. They are meant to do so. But they are no more ludicrous than life itself. And they illustrate in the most workaday fashion how you can test whether your literature fulfils its function of informing and transforming your existence.

I say that if daily events and scenes do not constantly recall and utilise the ideas and emotions contained in the books which you have read or are reading; if the memory of these books does not quicken the perception of beauty, wherever you happen to be, does not help you to correlate the particular trifle with the universal, does not smooth out irritation and give dignity to sorrow—then you are, consciously or not, unworthy of your high vocation as a bookman. You may say that I am preaching a sermon. The fact is, I am. My mood is a severely moral mood. For when I reflect upon the difference between what books have to offer and what even relatively earnest readers take the trouble to accept from them, I am appalled (or should be appalled, did I not know that the world is moving) by the sheer inefficiency, the bland, complacent failure of the earnest reader. I am like yourself, the spectacle of inefficiency rouses my holy ire.

Before you begin upon another masterpiece, set out in a row the masterpieces which you are proud of having read during the past year. Take the first on the list, that book which you perused in all the zeal of your New Year resolutions for systematic study. Examine the compartments of your mind. Search for the ideas and emotions which you have garnered from that book. Think, and recollect when last something from that book recurred to your memory apropos of your own daily commerce with humanity. Is it history—when did it throw a light for you on modern politics? Is it science—when did it show you order in apparent disorder, and help you to put two and two together into an inseparable four? Is it ethics—when did it influence your conduct in a twopenny-halfpenny affair between man and man? Is it a novel—when did it help you to "understand all and forgive all"? Is it poetry—when was it a magnifying glass to disclose beauty to you, or a fire to warm your cooling faith? If you can answer these questions satisfactorily, your stocktaking as regards the fruit of your traffic with that book may be reckoned satisfactory. If you cannot answer them satisfactorily, then either you chose the book badly or your impression that you *read* it is a mistaken one.

When the result of this stocktaking forces you to the conclusion that your riches are not so vast as you thought them to be, it is necessary to look about for the causes of the misfortune. The causes may be several. You may have been reading worthless books. This, however, I should say at once, is extremely unlikely. Habitual and confirmed readers, unless they happen to be reviewers, seldom read worthless books. In the first place, they are so busy with books of proved value that they have only a small margin of leisure left for very modern works, and generally, before they can catch up with the age, Time or the critic has definitely threshed for them the wheat from the chaff. No! Mediocrity has not much chance of hood-winking the serious student.

It is less improbable that the serious student has been choosing his books badly. He may do this in two ways—absolutely and relatively. Every reader of long standing has been through the singular experience of suddenly *seeing* a book with which his eyes have been familiar for years. He reads a book with a reputation and thinks: "Yes, this is a good book. This book gives me pleasure." And then after an interval, perhaps after half a lifetime, something mysterious happens to his mental sight. He picks up the book again, and sees a new and profound significance in every sentence, and he says: "I was perfectly blind to this book before." Yet he is no cleverer than he used to be. Only something has happened to him. Let a gold watch be discovered by a supposititious man who has never heard of watches. He has a sense of beauty. He admires the watch, and takes pleasure in it. He says: "This is a beautiful piece of bric-à-brac; I fully appreciate this delightful trinket." Then imagine his feelings when someone comes along with the key; imagine the light flooding his brain. Similar incidents occur in the eventful life of the constant reader. He has no key, and never suspects that there exists such a thing as a key. That is what I call a choice absolutely bad.

The choice is relatively bad when, spreading over a number of books, it pursues no order, and thus results in a muddle of faint impressions each blurring the rest. Books must be allowed to help one another; they must be skilfully called in to each other's aid. And that this may be accomplished some guiding principle is necessary. "And what," you demand, "should that guiding principle be?" How do I know? Nobody, fortunately, can make your principles for you. You have to make them for yourself. But I will venture upon this general observation: that in the mental world what counts is not numbers but co-ordination. As regards facts and ideas, the great mistake made by the average well-intentioned reader is that he is content with the names of things instead of occupying himself with the causes of things. He seeks answers to the question What? instead of to the question Why? He studies history, and never guesses that all history is caused by the facts of geography. He is a botanical expert, and can take you to where the *Sibthorpia europæa* grows, and never troubles to wonder what the earth would be without its cloak of plants. He wanders forth of starlit evenings and will name you with unction all the constellations from Andromeda to the Scorpion; but if you ask him why Venus can never be seen at midnight, he will tell you that he has not bothered with the scientific details. He has not learned that names are nothing, and the satisfaction of the lust of the eye a trifle compared to the imaginative vision of which scientific "details" are the indispensable basis.

Most reading, I am convinced, is unphilosophical; that is to say, it lacks the element which more than anything else quickens the poetry of life. Unless and until a man has formed a scheme of knowledge, be it a mere skeleton, his reading must necessarily be unphilosophical. He must have attained to some notion of the inter-relations of the various branches of knowledge before he can properly comprehend the branch in which he specialises. If he has not drawn an outline map upon which he can fill in whatever knowledge comes to him, as it comes, and on which he can trace the affinity of every part with every other part, he is assuredly frittering away a large percentage of his efforts. There are certain philosophical works which, once they are mastered, seem to have performed an operation for cataract, so that he who was blind, having read them, henceforward sees cause and effect working in and out everywhere. To use another figure, they leave stamped on the brain a chart of the entire province of knowledge.

Such a work is Spencer's *First Principles*. I know that it is nearly useless to advise people to read *First Principles*. They are intimidated by the sound of it; and it costs as much as a dress-circle seat at the theatre. But if they would, what brilliant stocktakings there might be in a few years! Why, if they would only read such detached essays as that on "Manners and Fashion," or "The Genesis of Science" (in a sixpenny volume of Spencer's *Essays*, published by Watts and Co.), the magic illumination, the necessary power of "synthetising" things, might be vouch-safed to them. In any case, the lack of some such disciplinary, co-ordinating measure will amply explain many disastrous stocktakings. The manner in which one single ray of light, one single precious hint, will clarify and energise the whole mental life of him who receives it, is among the most wonderful and heavenly of intellectual phenomena. Some men search for that light and never find it. But most men never search for it.

The superlative cause of disastrous stocktakings remains, and it is much more simple than the one with which I have just dealt. It consists in the absence of meditation. People read, and read, and read, blandly unconscious of their effrontery in assuming that they can assimilate without any further effort the vital essence which the author has breathed into them. They cannot. And the proof that they do not is shown all the time in their lives. I say that if a man does not spend at least as much time in actively and definitely thinking about what he has read as he has spent in reading, he is simply insulting his author. If he does not submit himself to intellectual and emotional fatigue in classifying the communicated ideas, and in emphasising on his spirit the imprint of the communicated emotions—then reading with him is a pleasant pastime and nothing else. This is a distressing fact. But it is a fact. It is distressing, for the reason that meditation is not a popular exercise. If a friend asks you what you did last night, you may answer, "I was reading," and he will be impressed and you will be proud. But if you answer, "I was meditating," he will have a tendency to smile and you will have a tendency to blush. I know this. I feel it myself. (I cannot offer any explanation.) But it does not shake my conviction that the absence of meditation is the main origin of disappointing stocktakings

THE FEAST OF ST. FRIEND

A CHRISTMAS BOOK

1911

* * * * *

ONE.

THE FACT

Something has happened to Christmas, or to our hearts; or to both. In order to be convinced of this it is only necessary to compare the present with the past. In the old days of not so long ago the festival began to excite us in November. For weeks the house rustled with charming and thrilling secrets, and with the furtive noises of paper parcels being wrapped and unwrapped; the house was a whispering gallery. The tension of expectancy increased to such a point that there was a positive danger of the cord snapping before it ought to snap. On the Eve we went to bed with no hope of settled sleep. We knew that we should be wakened and kept awake by the waits singing in the cold; and we were glad to be kept awake so. On the supreme day we came downstairs hiding delicious yawns, and cordially pretending that we had never been more fit. The day was different from other days; it had a unique romantic quality, tonic, curative of all ills. On that day even the tooth-ache vanished, retiring far into the wilderness with the spiteful word, the venomous thought, and the unlovely gesture. We sang with gusto "Christians awake, salute the happy morn." We did salute the happy morn. And when all the parcels were definitely unpacked, and the secrets of all hearts disclosed, we spent the rest of the happy morn in waiting, candidly greedy, for the first of the great meals. And then we ate, and we drank, and we ate again; with no thought of nutrition, nor of reasonableness, nor of the morrow, nor of dyspepsia. We ate and drank without fear and without shame, in the sheer, abandoned ecstasy of celebration. And by means of motley paper headgear, fit only for a carnival, we disguised ourselves in the most absurd fashions, and yet did not make ourselves seriously ridiculous; for ridicule is in the vision, not in what is seen. And we danced and sang and larked, until we could no more. And finally we chanted a song of ceremony, and separated; ending the day as we had commenced it, with salvoes of good wishes. And the next morning we were indisposed and enfeebled; and we did not care; we suffered gladly; we had our pain's worth, and more. This was the past.

* * * * *

Even today the spirit and rites of ancient Christmas are kept up, more or less in their full rigour and splendour, by a race of beings that is scattered over the whole earth. This race, mysterious, masterful, conservative, imaginative, passionately sincere, arriving from we know not where, dissolving before our eyes we know not how, has its way in spite of us. I mean the children. By virtue of the children's faith, the reindeer are still tramping the sky, and Christmas Day is still something above and beyond a day of the week; it is a day out of the week. We have to sit and pretend; and with disillusion in our souls we do pretend. At Christmas, it is not the children who make-believe; it is ourselves. Who does not remember the first inkling of a suspicion that Christmas Day was after all a day rather like any other day? In the house of my memories, it was the immemorial duty of my brother on Christmas morning, before anything else whatever happened, to sit down to the organ and perform "Christians Awake" with all possible stops drawn. He had to do it. Tradition, and the will that emanated from the best bedroom, combined to force him to do it. One Christmas morning, as he was preparing the stops, he glanced aside at me with a supercilious curl of the lips, and the curl of my lips silently answered. It was as if he had said: "I condescend to this," and as if I had said: "So do I."

Such a moment comes to most of us of this generation. And thenceforward the change in us is extraordinarily rapid. The next thing we know is that the institution of waits is a rather annoying survival which at once deprives us of sleep and takes money out of our pockets. And then Christmas is gluttony and indigestion and expensiveness and quarter-day, and Christmas cards are a tax and a nuisance, and present-giving is a heavier tax and a nuisance. And we feel self-conscious and foolish as we sing "Auld Lang Syne." And what a blessing it will be when the "festivities" (as they are misleadingly called) are over, and we can settle down into commonsense again!

* * * * *

I do not mean that our hearts are black with despair on Christmas Day. I do not mean that we do not enjoy ourselves on Christmas Day. There is no doubt that, with the inspiriting help of the mysterious race, and by the force of tradition, and by our own gift of pretending, we do still very much enjoy ourselves on Christmas Day. What I mean to insinuate, and to assert, is that beneath this enjoyment is the disconcerting and distressing conviction of unreality, of non-significance, of exaggerated and even false sentiment. What I mean is that we have to brace and force ourselves up to the enjoyment of Christmas. We have to induce deliberately the "Christmas feeling." We have to remind ourselves that "it will never do" to let the heartiness of Christmas be impaired. The peculiarity of our attitude towards Christmas, which at worst is a vacation, may be clearly seen by contrasting it with our attitude towards another vacation—the summer holiday. We do not have to brace and force ourselves up to the enjoyment of the summer holiday. We experience no difficulty in inducing the holiday feeling. There is no fear of the institution of the summer holiday losing its heartiness. Nor do we need the example of children to aid us in savouring the August "festivities."

* * * * *

If any person here breaks in with the statement that I am deceived and the truth is not in me, and that Christmas stands just where it did in the esteem of all right-minded people, and that he who casts a doubt on the heartiness of Christmas is not right-minded, let that person read no more. This book is not written for him. And if any other person, kindlier, condescendingly protests that there is nothing wrong with Christmas except my advancing age, let that person read no more. This book is not written for him, either. It is written for persons who can look facts cheerfully in the face. That Christmas has lost some of its magic is a fact that the common sense of the western hemisphere will not dispute. To blink the fact is infantile. To confront it, to try to understand it, to reckon with it, and to obviate any evil that may attach to it—this course alone is meet for an honest man.

* * * * *

TWO.

THE REASON

If the decadence of Christmas were a purely subjective phenomenon, confined to the breasts of those of us who have ceased to be children then it follows that Christmas has always been decadent, because people have always been ceasing to be children. It follows also that the festival was originally got up by disillusioned adults, for the benefit of the children. Which is totally absurd. Adults have never yet invented any institution, festival or diversion specially for the benefit of children. The egoism of adults makes such an effort impossible, and the ingenuity and pliancy of children make it unnecessary. The pantomime, for example, which is now pre-eminently a diversion for children, was created by adults for the amusement of adults. Children have merely accepted it and appropriated it. Children, being helpless, are of course fatalists and imitators. They take what comes, and they do the best they can with it. And when they have made something their own that was adult, they stick to it like leeches.

They are terrific Tories, are children; they are even reactionary! They powerfully object to changes. What they most admire in a pantomime is the oldest part of it, the only true pantomime—the harlequinade! Hence the very nature of children is a proof that what Christmas is now to them, it was in the past to their elders. If they now feel and exhibit faith and enthusiasm in the practice of the festival, be sure that, at one time, adults felt and exhibited the same faith and enthusiasm—yea, and more! For in neither faith nor enthusiasm can a child compete with a convinced adult. No child could believe in anything as passionately as the modern millionaire believes in money, or as the modern social reformer believes in the virtue of Acts of Parliament.

Another and a crowning proof that Christmas has been diminished in our hearts lies in the fiery lyrical splendour of the old Christmas hymns. Those hymns were not written by people who made-believe at Christmas for the pleasure of youngsters. They were written by devotees. And this age could not have produced them.

* * * * *

No! The decay of the old Christmas spirit among adults is undeniable, and its cause is fairly plain. It is due to the labours of a set of idealists— men who cared not for money, nor for glory, nor for anything except their ideal. Their ideal was to find out the truth concerning nature and concerning human history; and they sacrificed all—they sacrificed the peace of mind of whole generations—to the pleasure of slaking their ardour for truth. For them the most important thing in the world was the satisfaction of their curiosity. They would leave naught alone; and they scorned consequences. Useless to cry to them: "That is holy. Touch it not!" I mean the great philosophers and men of science—especially the geologists—of the nineteenth century. I mean such utterly pure-minded men as Lyell, Spencer, Darwin and Huxley. They inaugurated the mighty age of doubt and scepticism. They made it impossible to believe all manner of things which before them none had questioned. The movement spread until uneasiness was everywhere in the realm of thought, and people walked about therein fearsomely, as in a land subject to earthquakes. It was as if people had said: "We don't know what will topple next. Let's raze everything to the ground, and then we shall feel safer." And there came a moment after which nobody could ever look at a picture of the Nativity in the old way. Pictures of the Nativity were admired perhaps as much as ever, but for the exquisite beauty of their naïveté, the charm of their old-world simplicity, not as artistic renderings of fact.

* * * * *

An age of scepticism has its faults, like any other age, though certain persons have pretended the contrary. Having been compelled to abandon its belief in various statements of alleged fact, it lumps principles and ideals with alleged facts, and hastily decides not to believe in anything at all. It gives up faith, it despises faith, in spite of the warning of its greatest philosophers, including Herbert Spencer, that faith of some sort is necessary to a satisfactory existence in a universe full of problems which science admits it can never solve. None were humbler than the foremost scientists about the narrowness of the field of knowledge, as compared with the immeasurability of the field of faith. But the warning has been ignored, as warnings nearly always are. Faith is at a discount. And the qualities which go with faith are at a discount; such as enthusiasm, spontaneity, ebullition, lyricism, and self-expression in general. Sentimentality is held in such horror that people are afraid even of sentiment. Their secret cry is: "Give us something in which we can believe."

* * * * *

They forget, in their confusion, that the great principles, spiritual and moral, remain absolutely intact. They forget that, after all the shattering discoveries of science and conclusions of philosophy, mankind has still to live with dignity amid hostile nature, and in the presence of an unknowable power and that mankind can only succeed in this tremendous feat by the exercise of faith and of that mutual goodwill which is based in sincerity and charity. They forget that, while facts are nothing, these principles are everything. And so, at that epoch of the year which nature herself has ordained for the formal recognition of the situation of mankind in the universe and of its resulting duties to itself and to the Unknown—at that epoch, they bewail, sadly or impatiently or cynically: "Oh! The bottom has been knocked out of Christmas!"

* * * * *

But the bottom has not been knocked out of Christmas. And people know it. Somewhere, in the most central and mysterious fastness of their hearts, they know it. If they were not, in spite of themselves, convinced of it, why should they be so pathetically anxious to keep alive in themselves, and to foster in their children, the Christmas spirit? Obviously, a profound instinct is for ever reminding them that, without the Christmas spirit, they are lost. The forms of faith change, but the spirit of faith, which is the Christmas spirit, is immortal amid its endless vicissitudes. At a crisis of change, faith is weakened for the majority; for the majority it may seem to be dead. It is conserved, however, in the hearts of the few supremely great and in the hearts of the simple. The supremely great are hidden from the majority; but the simple are seen of all men, and them we encourage, often without knowing why, to be the depositaries of that which we cannot ourselves guard, but which we dimly feel to be indispensable to our safety.

* * * * *

THREE.

THE SOLSTICE AND GOOD WILL

In order to see that there is underlying Christmas an idea of faith which will at any rate last as long as the planet lasts, it is only necessary to ask and answer the question: "Why was the Christmas feast fixed for the twenty-fifth of December?" For it is absolutely certain, and admitted by everybody of knowledge, that Christ was not born on the twenty-fifth of December. Those disturbing impassioned inquirers after truth, who will not leave us peaceful in our ignorance, have settled that for us, by pointing out, among other things, that the twenty-fifth of December falls in the very midst of the Palestine rainy season, and that, therefore, shepherds were assuredly not on that date watching their flocks by night.

* * * * *

Christians were not, at first, united in the celebration of Christmas. Some kept Christmas in January, others in April, others in May. It was a pre-Christian force which drove them all into agreement upon the twenty-fifth of December. Just as they wisely took the Christmas tree from the Roman Saturnalia, so they took the date of their festival from the universal pre-Christian festival of the winter solstice, Yule, when mankind celebrated the triumph of the sun over the powers of darkness, when the night begins to decrease and the day to increase, when the year turns, and hope is born again because the worst is over. No more suitably symbolic moment could have been chosen for a festival of faith, goodwill and joy. And the appositeness of the moment is just as perfect in this era of electric light and central heating, as it was in the era of Virgil, who, by the way, described a Christmas tree. We shall say this year, with exactly the same accents of relief and hope as our pagan ancestors used, and as the woaded savage used: "The days will begin to lengthen now!" For, while we often falsely fancy that we have subjugated nature to our service, the fact is that we are as irremediably as ever at the mercy of nature.

* * * * *

Indeed, the attitude of us moderns towards the forces by which our existence is governed ought to be, and probably is, more reverent and awe-struck than that of the earlier world. The discoveries of science have at once quickened our imagination and compelled us to admit that what we know is the merest trifle. The pagan in his ignorance explained everything. Our knowledge has only deepened the mystery, and all that we shall learn will but deepen it further. We can explain the solstice. We are aware with absolute certitude that the solstice and the equinox and the varying phenomena of the seasons are due to the fact that the plane of the equator is tilted at a slight angle to the plane of the ecliptic. When we put on the first overcoat in autumn, and when we give orders to let the furnace out in spring, we know that we are arranging our lives in accordance with that angle. And we are quite duly proud of our knowledge. And much good does our knowledge do us!

* * * * *

Well, it does do us some good, and in a spiritual way, too! For nobody can even toy with astronomy without picturing to himself, more clearly and startlingly than would be otherwise possible, a revolving globe that whizzes through elemental space around a ball of fire: which, in turn, is rushing with all its satellites at an inconceivable speed from nowhere to nowhere; and to the surface of the revolving, whizzing globe a multitude of living things desperately clinging, and these living things, in the midst of cataclysmic danger, and between the twin enigmas of birth and death, quarrelling and hating and calling themselves kings and queens and millionaires and beautiful women and aristocrats and geniuses and lackeys and superior persons! Perhaps the highest value of astronomy is that it renders more vivid the ironical significance of such a vision, and thus brings home to us the truth that in spite of all the differences which we have invented, mankind is a fellowship of brothers, overshadowed by insoluble and fearful mysteries, and dependent upon mutual goodwill and trust for the happiness it may hope to achieve. * * * Let us remember that Christmas is, among other things, the winter solstice, and that the bottom has not yet been knocked out of the winter solstice, nor is likely to be in the immediate future!

* * * * *

It is a curious fact that the one faith which really does flourish and wax in these days should be faith in the idea of social justice. For social justice simply means the putting into practice of goodwill and the recognition of the brotherhood of mankind. Formerly, people were enthusiastic and altruistic for a theological idea, for a national idea, for a political idea. You could see men on the rack for the sake of a dogma; you could see men of a great nation fitting out regiments and ruining themselves and going forth to save a small nation from destruction. You could see men giving their lives to the aggrandisement of an empire. And the men who did these things had the best brains and the quickest wits and the warmest hearts of their time. But today, whenever you meet a first-class man who is both enthusiastic and altruistic, you may be sure that his pet scheme is neither theological, military nor political; you may be sure that he has got into his head the notion that some class of persons somewhere are not being treated fairly, are not being treated with fraternal goodwill, and that he is determined to put the matter right, or perish.

* * * * *

In England, nearly all the most interesting people are social reformers: and the only circles of society in which you are not bored, in which there is real conversation, are the circles of social reform. These people alone have an abounding and convincing faith. Their faith has, for example, convinced many of the best literary artists of the day, with the result that a large proportion of the best modern imaginative literature has been inspired by the dream of social justice. Take away that idea from the works of H.G. Wells, John Galsworthy and George Bernard Shaw, and there would be exactly nothing left. Despite any appearance to the contrary, therefore, the idea of universal goodwill is really alive upon the continents of this planet: more so, indeed, than any other idea—for the vitality of an idea depends far less on the numbers of people who hold it than on the quality of the heart and brain of the people who hold it. Whether the growth of the idea is due to the spiritual awe and humility which are the consequence of increased scientific knowledge, I cannot say, and I do not seriously care.

* * * * *

FOUR.

THE APPOSITENESS OF CHRISTMAS

"Yes," you say, "I am quite at one with you as to the immense importance of goodwill in social existence, and I have the same faith in it as you have. But why a festival? Why eating and drinking and ceremonies? Surely one can have faith without festivals?"

* * * * *

The answer is that one cannot; or at least that in practice, one never does. A disinclination for festivals, a morbid self-conscious fear of letting oneself go, is a sure sign of lack of faith. If you have not enough enthusiasm for the cult of goodwill to make you positively desire to celebrate the cult, then your faith is insufficient and needs fostering by study and meditation. Why, if you decide to found a sailing-club up your creek, your very first thought is to signalise your faith in the sailing of those particular waters by a dinner and a jollity, and you take care that the event shall be an annual one! * * * You have faith in your wife, and in your affection for her. Surely you don't need a festival to remind you of that faith, you so superior to human weaknesses? But you do! You insist on having it. And, if the festival did not happen, you would feel gloomy and discouraged. A birthday is a device for recalling to you in a formal and impressive manner that a certain person still lives and is in need of goodwill. It is a device which experience has proved to be both valuable and necessary.

* * * * *

Real faith effervesces; it shoots forth in every direction; it communicates itself. And the inevitable result is a festival. The festival is anticipated with pleasure, and it is remembered with pleasure. And thus it reacts stimulatingly on that which gave it birth, as the vitality of children reacts stimulatingly on the vitality of parents. It provides a concrete symbol of that which is invisible and intangible, and mankind is not yet so advanced in the path of spiritual perfection that we can afford to dispense with concrete symbols. Now, if we maintain festivals and formalities for the healthy continuance and honour of a pastime or of a personal affection, shall we not maintain a festival—and a mighty one—in behalf of a faith which makes the corporate human existence bearable amid the menaces and mysteries that for ever threaten it,—the faith of universal goodwill and mutual confidence?

* * * * *

If then, there is to be a festival, why should it not be the festival of Christmas? It can, indeed, be no other. Christmas is most plainly indicated. It is dignified and made precious by traditions which go back much further than the Christian era; and it has this tremendous advantage—it exists! In spite of our declining faith, it has been preserved to us, and here it is, ready to hand. Not merely does it fall at the point which uncounted generations have agreed to consider as the turn of the solar year and as the rebirth of hope! It falls also immediately before the end of the calendar year, and thus prepares us for a fresh beginning that shall put the old to shame. It could not be better timed. Further, its traditional spirit of peace and goodwill is the very spirit which we desire to foster. And finally its customs—or at any rate, its main customs—are well designed to symbolize that spirit. If we have allowed the despatch of Christmas cards to degenerate into naught but a tedious shuffling of paste-boards and overwork of post-office officials, the fault is not in the custom but in ourselves. The custom is a most striking one—so long as we have sufficient imagination to remember vividly that we are all in the same boat—I mean, on the same planet—and clinging desperately to the flying ball, and dependent for daily happiness on one another's good will! A Christmas card sent by one human being to another human being is more than a piece of coloured stationery sent by one log of wood to another log of wood: it is an inspiring and reassuring message of high value. The mischief is that so many self-styled human beings are just logs of wood, rather stylishly dressed.

* * * * *

And then the custom of present-giving! What better and more convincing proof of sympathy than a gift? The gift is one of these obvious contrivances—like the wheel or the lever—which smooth and simplify earthly life, and the charm of whose utility no obviousness can stale. But of course any contrivance can be rendered futile by clumsiness or negligence. There is a sort of Christmas giver who says pettishly: "Oh! I don't know what to give to So-and-So this Christmas! What a bother! I shall write and tell her to choose something herself, and send the bill to me!" And he writes. And though he does not suspect it, what he really writes, and what So-and-So reads, is this: "Dear So-and-So. It is nothing to me that you and I are alive together on this planet, and in various ways mutually dependent. But I am bound by custom to give you a present. I do not, however, take sufficient interest in your life to know what object it would give you pleasure to possess; and I do not want to be put to the trouble of finding out, nor of obtaining the object and transmitting it to you. Will you, therefore, buy something for yourself and send the bill to me. Of course, a sense of social decency will prevent you from spending more than a small sum, and I shall be spared all exertion beyond signing a cheque. Yours insincerely and loggishly * * *." So managed, the contrivance of present-giving becomes positively sinister in its working. But managed with the sympathetic imagination which is infallibly produced by real faith in goodwill, its efficacy may approach the miraculous.

* * * * *

The Christmas ceremony of good-wishing by word of mouth has never been in any danger of falling into insincerity. Such is the power of tradition and virtue of a festival, and such the instinctive brotherliness of men, that on this day the mere sight of an acquaintance will soften the voice and warm the heart of the most superior sceptic and curmudgeon that the age of disillusion has produced. In spite of himself, faith flickers up in him again, be it only for a moment. And, during that moment, he is almost like those whose bright faith the age has never tarnished, like the great and like the simple, to whom it is quite unnecessary to offer a defence and explanation of Christmas or to suggest the basis of a new faith therein.

* * * * *

FIVE.

DEFENCE OF FEASTING

And now I can hear the superior sceptic disdainfully questioning: "Yes, but what about the orgy of Christmas? What about all the eating and drinking?" To which I can only answer that faith causes effervescence, expansion, joy, and that joy has always, for excellent reasons, been connected with feasting. The very words 'feast' and 'festival' are etymologically inseparable. The meal is the most regular and the least dispensable of daily events; it happens also to be an event which is in itself almost invariably a source of pleasure, or, at worst, of satisfaction: and it will continue to have this precious quality so long as our souls are encased in bodies. What could be more natural, therefore, than that it should be employed, with due enlargement and ornamentation, as the kernel of the festival? What more logical than that the meal should be elevated into a feast?

"But," exclaims the superior sceptic, "this idea involves the idea of excess!" What if it does? I would not deny it! Assuredly, a feast means more than enough, and more than enough means excess. It is only because a feast means excess that it assists in the bringing about of expansion and joy. Such is human nature, and it is the case of human nature that we are discussing. Of course, excess usually exacts its toll, within twenty-four hours, especially from the weak. But the benefit is worth its price. The body pays no more than the debt which the soul has incurred. An occasional change of habit is essential to well-being, and every change of habit results in temporary derangement and inconvenience.

Do not misunderstand me. Do not push my notion of excess to extremes. When I defend the excess inevitably incident to a feast, I am not seeking to prove that a man in celebrating Christmas is entitled to drink champagne in a public restaurant until he becomes an object of scorn and disgust to the waiters who have travelled from Switzerland in order to receive his tips. Much less should I be prepared to justify him if, in his own home, he sank lower than the hog. Nor would I sympathetically carry him to bed. There is such a thing as excess in moderation and dignity. Every wise man has practised this. And he who has not practised it is a fool, and deserves even a harder name. He ought indeed to inhabit a planet himself, for all his faith in humanity will be exhausted in believing in himself. * * * So much for the feast!

* * * * *

But the accompaniments of the feast are also excessive. For example, you make a tug-of-war with your neighbour at table, and the rope is a fragile packet of tinselled paper, which breaks with a report like a pistol. You open your half of the packet, and discover some doggerel verse which you read aloud, and also a perfectly idiotic coloured cap, which you put on your head to the end of looking foolish. And this ceremony is continued until the whole table is surrounded by preposterous headgear, and doggerel verse is lying by every plate. Surely no man in his senses, no woman in hers, would, etc., etc. * * *! But one of the spiritual advantages of feasting is that it expands you beyond your common sense. One excess induces another, and a finer one. This acceptance of the ridiculous is good for you. It is particularly good for an Anglo-Saxon, who is so self-contained and self-controlled that his soul might stiffen as the unused limb of an Indian fakir stiffens, were it not for periodical excitements like that of the Christmas feast. Everybody has experienced the self-conscious reluctance which precedes the putting on of the cap, and the relief, followed by further expansion and ecstasy, which ensues after the putting on. Everybody who has put on a cap is aware that it is a beneficial thing to put on a cap. Quite apart from the fact that the mysterious and fanciful race of children are thereby placated and appeased, the soul of the capped one is purified by this charming excess.

* * * * *

And the Tree! What an excess of the fantastic to pretend that all those glittering balls, those coloured candles and those variegated parcels are the blossoms of the absurd tree! How excessively grotesque to tie all those parcels to the branches, in order to take them off again! Surely, something less medieval, more ingenious, more modern than this could be devised—if symbolism is to be indulged in at all! Can you devise it, O sceptical one, revelling in disillusion? Can you invent a symbol more natural and graceful than the symbol of the Tree? Perhaps you would have a shop-counter, and shelves behind it, so as to instill early into the youthful mind that this is a planet of commerce! Perhaps you would abolish the doggerel of crackers, and substitute therefor extracts from the Autobiography of Benjamin Franklin! Perhaps you would exchange the caps for blazonry embroidered with chemical formula, your object being the advancement of science! Perhaps you would do away with the orgiastic eating and drinking, and arrange for a formal conversation about astronomy and the idea of human fraternity, upon strictly reasonable rations of shredded wheat! You would thus create an original festival, and eliminate all fear of a dyspeptic morrow. You would improve the mind. And you would avoid the ridiculous. But also, in avoiding the ridiculous, you would tumble into the ridiculous, deeply and hopelessly! And think how your very original festival would delight the participators, how they would look forward to it with joy, and back upon it with pleasurable regret; how their minds would dwell sweetly upon the conception of shredded wheat, and how their faith would be encouraged and strengthened by the intellectuality of the formal conversation!

* * * * *

He who girds at an ancient established festival should reflect upon sundry obvious truths before he withers up the said festival by the sirocco of his contempt. These truths are as follows:—First, a festival, though based upon intelligence, is not an affair of the intellect, but an affair of the emotions. Second, the human soul can only be reached through the human body. Third, it is impossible to replace an ancient festival by a new one. Robespierre, amongst others, tried to do so, and achieved the absurd. Reformers, heralds of new faiths, and rejuvenators of old faiths, have always, when they succeeded, adopted an ancient festival, with all or most of its forms, and been content to breathe into it a new spirit to replace the old spirit which had vanished or was vanishing. Anybody who, persuaded that Christmas is not what it was, feels that a festival must nevertheless be preserved, will do well to follow this example. To be content with the old forms and to vitalize them: that is the problem. Solve it, and the forms will soon begin to adapt themselves to the process of vitalization. All history is a witness in proof.

* * * * *

SIX.

TO REVITALIZE THE FESTIVAL

It being agreed, then, that the Christmas festival has lost a great deal of its old vitality, and that, to many people, it is a source of tedium and the cause of insincerity; and it being further agreed that the difficulty cannot be got over by simply abolishing the festival, as no one really wants it to be abolished; the question remains—what should be done to vitalize it? The former spirit of faith, the spirit which made the great Christmas of the golden days, has been weakened; but one element of it—that which is founded on the conviction that goodwill among men is a prime necessity of reasonable living—survives with a certain vigour, though even it has not escaped the general scepticism of the age. This element unites in agreement all the pugnacious sectaries who join battle over the other elements of the former faith. This element has no enemies. None will deny its lasting virtue. Obviously, therefore, the right course is to concentrate on the cultivation of goodwill. If goodwill can be consciously increased, the festival of Christmas will cease to be perfunctory. It will acquire a fresh and more genuine significance, which, however, will not in any way inconvenience those who have never let go of the older significance. No tradition will be overthrown, no shock administered, and nobody will be able to croak about iconoclasm and new-fangled notions and the sudden end of the world, and so on.

* * * * *

The fancy of some people will at once run to the formation of a grand international Society for the revivifying of Christmas by the cultivation of goodwill, with branches in all the chief cities of Europe and America, and headquarters—of course at the Hague; and committees and subcommittees, and presidents and vice-presidents; and honorary secretaries and secretaries paid; and quarterly and annual meetings, and triennial congresses! And a literary organ or two! And a badge—naturally a badge, designed by a famous artist in harmonious tints!

* * * * *

But my fancy does not run at all in this direction. I am convinced that we have already far too many societies for the furtherance of our ends. To my mind, most societies with a moral aim are merely clumsy machines for doing simple jobs with the maximum of friction, expense and inefficiency. I should define the majority of these societies as a group of persons each of whom expects the others to do something very wonderful. Why create a society in order to help you to perform some act which nobody can perform but yourself? No society can cultivate goodwill in you. You might as well create a society for shaving or for saying your prayers. And further, goodwill is far less a process of performing acts than a process of thinking thoughts. To think, is it necessary to involve yourself in the cog-wheels of a society? Moreover, a society means fuss and shouting: two species of disturbance which are both futile and deleterious, particularly in an intimate affair of morals.

You can best help the general cultivation of goodwill along by cultivating goodwill in your own heart. Until you have started the task of personal cultivation, you will probably assume that there will be time left over for superintending the cultivation of goodwill in other people's hearts. But a very little experience ought to show you that this is a delusion. You will perceive, if not at once, later, that you have bitten off just about as much as you can chew. And you will appreciate also the wisdom of not advertising your enterprise. Why, indeed, should you breathe a word to a single soul concerning your admirable intentions? Rest assured that any unusual sprouting of the desired crop will be instantly noticed by the persons interested.

* * * * *

The next point is: Towards whom are you to cultivate goodwill? Naturally, one would answer: Towards the whole of humanity. But the whole of humanity, as far as you are concerned, amounts to naught but a magnificent abstract conception. And it is very difficult to cultivate goodwill towards a magnificent abstract conception. The object of goodwill ought to be clearly defined, and very visible to the physical eye, especially in the case of people, such as us, who are only just beginning to give to the cultivation of goodwill, perhaps, as much attention as we give to our clothes or our tobacco. If a novice sets out to embrace the whole of humanity in his goodwill, he will have even less success than a young man endeavouring to fall in love with four sisters at once; and his daily companions—those who see him eat his bacon and lace his boots and earn his living—will most certainly have a rough time of it. * * * No! It will be best for you to centre your efforts on quite a small group of persons, and let the rest of humanity struggle on as well as it can, with no more of your goodwill than it has hitherto had.

In choosing the small group of people, it will be unnecessary for you to go to Timbuktu, or into the next street or into the next house. And, in this group of people you will be wise, while neglecting no member of the group, to specialise on one member. Your wife, if you have one, or your husband? Not necessarily. I was meaning simply that one who most frequently annoys you. He may be your husband, or she may be your wife. These things happen. He may be your butler. Or you may be his butler. She may be your daughter, or he may be your father, and you a charming omniscient girl of seventeen wiser than anybody else. Whoever he or she may be who oftenest inspires you with a feeling of irritated superiority, aim at that person in particular.

The frequency of your early failures with him or her will show you how prudent you were not to make an attempt on the whole of humanity at once. And also you will see that you did well not to publish your excellent intentions. If nobody is aware of your striving, nobody will be aware that you have failed in striving. Your successes will appear effortless, and most important of all, you will be free from the horrid curse of self-consciousness. Herein is one of the main advantages of not wearing a badge. Lastly, you will have the satisfaction of feeling that, if everybody else is doing as you are, the whole of humanity is being attended to after all. And the comforting thought is that very probably, almost certainly, quite a considerable number of people are in fact doing as you are; some of them—make no doubt—are doing a shade better. I now come to the actual method of cultivating goodwill.

* * * * *

SEVEN.

THE GIFT OF ONESELF

Children divide their adult acquaintances into two categories—those who sympathise with them in the bizarre and trying adventure called life; and those who don't. The second category is much the larger of the two. Very many people belong to it who think that they belong to the first. They may deceive themselves, but they cannot deceive a child. Although you may easily practise upon the credulity of a child in matters of fact, you cannot cheat his moral and social judgment. He will add you up, and he will add anybody up, and he will estimate conduct, upon principles of his own and in a manner terribly impartial. Parents have no sterner nor more discerning critics than their own children.

And so you may be polite to a child, and pretend to appreciate his point of view; but, unless you really do put yourself to the trouble of understanding him, unless you throw yourself, by the exercise of imagination, into his world, you will not succeed in being his friend. To be his friend means an effort on your part, it means that you must divest yourself of your own mental habit, and, for the time being, adopt his. And no nice phrases, no gifts of money, sweets or toys, can take the place of this effort, and this sacrifice of self. With five minutes of genuine surrender to him, you can win more of his esteem and gratitude than five hundred pounds would buy. His notion of real goodwill is the imaginative sharing of his feelings, a convinced participation in his pains and pleasures. He is well aware that, if you honestly do this, you will be on his side.

* * * * *

Now, adults, of course, are tremendously clever and accomplished persons and children are no match for them; but still, with all their talents and omniscience and power, adults seem to lack important pieces of knowledge which children possess; they seem to forget, and to fail to profit by, their infantile experience. Else why should adults in general be so extraordinarily ignorant of the great truth that the secret of goodwill lies in the sympathetic exercise of the imagination? Since goodwill is the secret of human happiness, it follows that the secret of goodwill must be one of the most precious aids to sensible living; and yet adults, though they once knew it, have gone and forgotten it! Children may well be excused for concluding that the ways of the adult, in their capricious irrationality, are past finding out.

To increase your goodwill for a fellow creature, it is necessary to imagine that you are he: and nothing else is necessary. This feat is not easy; but it can be done. Some people have less of the divine faculty of imagination than others, but nobody is without it, and, like all other faculties, it improves with use, just as it deteriorates with neglect. Imagination is a function of the brain. In order to cultivate goodwill for a person, you must think frequently about that person. You must inform yourself about all his activities. You must be able in your mind's eye to follow him hour by hour throughout the day, and you must ascertain if he sleeps well at night—because this is not a trifle. And you must reflect upon his existence with the same partiality as you reflect upon your own. (Why not?) That is to say, you must lay the fullest stress on his difficulties, disappointments and unhappinesses, and you must minimise his good fortune. You must magnify his efforts after righteousness, and forget his failures. You must ever remember that, after all, he is not to blame for

176

the faults of his character, which faults, in his case as in yours, are due partly to heredity and partly to environment. And beyond everything you must always give him credit for good intentions. Do not you, though sometimes mistakenly, always act for the best? You know you do! And are you alone among mortals in rectitude?

* * * * *

This mental exercise in relation to another person takes time, and it involves a fatiguing effort. I repeat that it is not easy. Nor is it invariably agreeable. You may, indeed, find it tedious, for example, to picture in vivid detail all the worries that have brought about your wife's exacerbation—negligent maid, dishonest tradesman, milk in a thunder storm, hypercritical husband, dirt in the wrong place—but, when you have faithfully done so, I absolutely defy you to speak to her in the same tone as you used to employ, and to cherish resentment against her as you used to do. And I absolutely defy you not to feel less discontented with yourself than in the past. It is impossible that the exercise of imagination about a person should not result in goodwill towards that person. The exercise may put a strain upon you; but its effect is a scientific certainty. It is the supreme social exercise, for it is the giving of oneself in the most intimate and complete sense. It is the suspension of one's individuality in favour of another. It establishes a new attitude of mind, which, though it may well lead to specific social acts, is more valuable than any specific act, for it is ceaselessly translating itself into demeanour.

* * * * *

The critic with that terrible English trait, an exaggerated sense of the ridiculous, will at this point probably remark to himself, smiling: "I suppose the time will come, when by dint of regular daily practice, I shall have achieved perfect goodwill towards the first object of my attentions. I can then regard that person as 'done.' I can put him on a shelf, and turn to the next; and, in the end, all my relations, friends and acquaintances will be 'done' and I can stare at them in a row on the shelf of my mind, with pride and satisfaction * * *." Except that no person will ever be quite "done," human nature, still being human, in spite of the recent advances of civilisation, I do not deprecate this manner of stating the case.

The ambitious and resolute man, with an exaggerated sense of the ridiculous, would see nothing ridiculous in ticking off a number of different objects as they were successively achieved. If for example it was part of his scheme to learn various foreign languages, he would know that he could only succeed by regular application of the brain, by concentration of thought daily; he would also know that he could never acquire any foreign language in absolute perfection. Still, he would reach a certain stage in a language, and then he would put it aside and turn to the next one on his programme, and so on. Assuredly, he would not be ashamed of employing method to reach his end.

Now all that can be said of the acquirement of foreign languages can be said of the acquirement of goodwill. In remedying the deficiences of the heart and character, as in remedying the deficiences of mere knowledge, the brain is the sole possible instrument, and the best results will be obtained by using it regularly and scientifically, according to an arranged method. Why, therefore, if a man be proud of method in improving his knowledge, should he see something ridiculous in a deliberate plan for improving his heart—the affair of his heart being immensely more important, more urgent and more difficult? The reader who has found even one good answer to the above question, need read no more of this book, for he will have confounded me and it.

* * * * *

EIGHT.

THE FEAST OF ST. FRIEND

The consequences of the social self-discipline which I have outlined will be various. A fairly early result will be the gradual decline, and ultimately the death, of the superior person in oneself. It is true that the superior person in oneself has nine lives, and is capable of rising from the dead after even the most fatal blows. But, at worst, the superior person—(and who among us does not shelter that sinister inhabitant in his soul?)—will have a very poor time in the soul of him who steadily practises the imaginative understanding of other people. In the first place, the mere exercise of the imagination on others absolutely scotches egotism as long as it lasts, and leaves it weakened afterwards. And, in the second and more important place, an improved comprehension of others (which means an intensified sympathy with them) must destroy the illusion, so widespread, that one's own case is unique. The amicable study of one's neighbours on the planet inevitably shows that the same troubles, the same fortitudes, the same feats of intelligence, the same successes and failures, are constantly happening everywhere. One can, indeed, see oneself in nearly everybody else, and, in particular, one is struck by the fact that the quality in which one took most pride is simply spread abroad throughout humanity in heaps! It is only in sympathetically contemplating others that one can get oneself in a true perspective. Yet probably the majority of human beings never do contemplate others, save with the abstracted gaze which proves that the gazer sees nothing but his own dream.

* * * * *

Another result of the discipline is an immensely increased interest in one's friends. One regards them even with a sort of proprietary interest, for, by imagination, one has come into sympathetic possession of them. Further, one has for them that tender feeling which always follows the conferring of a benefit, especially the secret conferring of a benefit. It is the benefactor, not the person benefited, who is grateful. The benefit which one has conferred is, of course, the gift of oneself. The resulting emotion is independent of any sympathy rendered by the other; and where the sympathy is felt to be mutual, friendship acquires a new significance. The exercise of sympathetic imagination will cause one to look upon even a relative as a friend—a startling achievement! It will provide a new excitement and diversion in life.

When the month of December dawns, there need be no sensation of weary apprehension about the difficulty of choosing a present that will suit a friend. Certainly it will not be necessary, from sheer indifference and ignorance, to invite the friend to choose his own present. On the contrary, one will be, in secret, so intimate with the friend's situation and wants and desires, that sundry rival schemes for pleasuring him will at once offer themselves. And when he receives the present finally selected, he will have the conviction, always delightfully flattering to a donee, that he has been the object of a particular attention and insight. * * * And when the cards of greeting are despatched, formal phrases will go forth charged, in the consciousness of the sender, with a genuine meaning, with the force of a climax, as though the sender had written thereon, in invisible ink: "I have had you well in mind during the last twelve months; I think I understand your difficulties and appreciate your efforts better than I did, and so it is with a peculiar sympathetic knowledge that I wish you good luck. I have guessed what particular kind of good luck you require, and I wish accordingly. My wish is not vague and perfunctory only."

* * * * *

And on the day of festival itself one feels that one really has something to celebrate. The occasion has a basis, if it had no basis for one before; and if a basis previously existed, then it is widened and strengthened. The festival becomes a public culmination to a private enterprise. One is not reminded by Christmas of goodwill, because the enterprise of imaginative sympathy has been a daily affair throughout the year; but Christmas provides an excuse for taking satisfaction in the success of the enterprise and new enthusiasm to correct its failures. The symbolism of the situation of Christmas, at the turn of the year, develops an added impressiveness, and all the Christmas customs, apt to produce annoyance in the breasts of the unsentimental, are accepted with indulgence, even with eagerness, because their symbolism also is shown in a clearer light. Christmas becomes as personal as a birthday. One eats and drinks to excess, not because it is the custom to eat and drink to excess, but from sheer effervescent faith in an idea. And as one sits with one's friends, possessing them in the privacy of one's heart, permeated by a sense of the value of sympathetic comprehension in this formidable adventure of existence on a planet that rushes eternally through the night of space; assured indeed that companionship and mutual understanding alone make the adventure agreeable,—one sees in a flash that Christmas, whatever else it may be, is and must be the Feast of St. Friend, and a day on that account supreme among the days of the year.

* * * * *

The third and greatest consequence of the systematic cultivation of goodwill now grows blindingly apparent. To state it earlier in all its crudity would have been ill-advised; and I purposely refrained from doing so. It is the augmentation of one's own happiness. The increase of amity, the diminution of resentment and annoyance, the regular maintenance of an attitude mildly benevolent towards mankind,—these things are the surest way to happiness. And it is because they are the surest way to happiness, that the most enlightened go after them. All real motives are selfish motives; were it otherwise humanity would be utterly different from what it is. A man may perform some act which will benefit another while working some striking injury to himself. But his reason for doing it is that he prefers the evil of the injury to the deeper evil of the fundamental dissatisfaction which would torment him if he did not perform the act. Nobody yet sought the good of another save as a means to his own good. And it is in accordance with common sense that this should be so. There is, however, a lower egotism and a higher. It is the latter which we call unselfishness. And it is the latter of which Christmas is the celebration. We shall legitimately bear in mind, therefore, that Christmas, in addition to being the Feast of St. Friend, is even more profoundly the feast of one's own welfare.

*   *   *   *   *

NINE.

THE REACTION

A reaction sets in between Christmas and the New Year. It is inevitable; and I should be writing basely if I did not devote to it a full chapter. In those few dark days of inactivity, between a fete and the resumption of the implacable daily round, when the weather is usually cynical, and we are paying in our tissues the fair price of excess, we see life and the world in a grey and sinister light, which we imagine to be the only true light. Take the case of the average successful man of thirty-five. What is he thinking as he lounges about on the day after Christmas?

His thoughts probably run thus: "Even if I live to a good old age, which is improbable, as many years lie behind me as before me. I have lived half my life, and perhaps more than half my life. I have realised part of my worldly ambition. I have made many good resolutions, and kept one or two of them in k more or less imperfect manner. I cannot, as a commonsense person, hope to keep a larger proportion of good resolutions in the future than I have kept in the past. I have tried to understand and sympathise with my fellow creatures, and though I have not entirely failed to do so, I have nearly failed. I am not happy and I am not content. And if, after all these years, I am neither happy nor content, what chance is there of my being happy and content in the second half of my life? The realisation of part of my worldly ambition has not made me any happier, and, therefore, it is unlikely that the realisation of the whole of my ambition will make me any happier. My strength cannot improve; it can only weaken; and my health likewise. I in my turn am coming to believe—what as a youth I rejected with disdain—namely, that happiness is what one is not, and content is what one has not. Why, then, should I go on striving after the impossible? Why should I not let things slide?"

Thus reflects the average successful man, and there is not one of us, successful or unsuccessful, ambitious or unambitious, whose reflections have not often led him to a conclusion equally dissatisfied. Why should I or anybody pretend that this is not so?

* * * * *

And yet, in the very moment of his discouragement and of his blackest vision of things, that man knows quite well that he will go on striving. He knows that his instinct to strive will be stronger than his genuine conviction that the desired end cannot be achieved. Positive though he may be that a worldly ambition realised will produce the same dissatisfaction as Dead Sea fruit in the mouth, he will still continue to struggle. * * * Now you cannot argue against facts, and this is a fact. It must be accepted. Conduct must be adjusted to it. The struggle being inevitable, it must be carried through as well as it can be carried through. It will not end brilliantly, but precautions can be taken against it ending disgracefully. These precautions consist in the devising of a plan of campaign, and the plan of campaign is defined by a series of resolutions: which resolutions are generally made at or immediately before the beginning of a New Year. Without these the struggle would be formless, confused, blind and even more futile than it is with them. Organised effort is bound to be less ineffective than unorganised effort.

* * * * *

A worldly ambition can be, frequently is, realised: but an ideal cannot be attained—if it could, it would not be an ideal. The virtue of an ideal is its unattainability. It seems, when it is first formed, just as attainable as a worldly ambition which indeed is often schemed as a means to it. After twenty-four hours, the ideal is all but attained. After forty-eight, it is a little farther off. After a week, it has receded still further. After a month it is far away; and towards the end of a year even the keen eye of hope has almost lost sight of it; it is definitely withdrawn from the practical sphere. And then, such is the divine obstinacy of humanity, the turn of the year gives us an excuse for starting afresh, and forming a new ideal, and forgetting our shame in yet another organised effort. Such is the annual circle of the ideal, the effort, the failure and the shame. A rather pitiful history it may appear! And yet it is also rather a splendid history! For the failure and the shame are due to the splendour of our ideal and to the audacity of our faith in ourselves. It is only in comparison with our ideal that we have fallen low. We are higher, in our failure and our shame, than we should have been if we had not attempted to rise.

* * * * *

There are those who will say: "At any rate, we might moderate somewhat the splendour of our ideal and the audacity of our self-conceit, so that there should be a less grotesque disparity between the aim and the achievement. Surely such moderation would be more in accord with common sense! Surely it would lessen the spiritual fatigue and disappointment caused by sterile endeavour!" It would. But just try to moderate the ideal and the self-conceit! And you will find, in spite of all your sad experiences, that you cannot. If there is the stuff of a man in you, you simply cannot! The truth, is that, in the supreme things, a man does not act under the rules of earthly common sense. He transcends them, because there is a quality in him which compels him to do so. Common sense may persuade him to attempt to keep down the ideal, and self-conceit may pretend to agree. But all the time, self-conceit will be whispering: "I can go one better than that." And lo! the ideal is furtively raised again.

A man really has little scientific control over the height of his ideal and the intensity of his belief in himself. He is born with them, as he is born with a certain pulse and a certain reflex action. He can neglect the ideal, so that it almost dissolves, but he cannot change its height. He can maim his belief in himself by persistent abandonment to folly, but he cannot lower its flame by an effort of the will, as he might lower the flame of a gas by a calculated turn of the hand. In the secret and inmost constitution of humanity it is ordained that the disparity between the aim and the achievement shall seem grotesque; it is ordained that there shall be an enormous fuss about pretty nearly nothing; it is ordained that the mountain shall bring forth a mouse. But it is also ordained that men shall go blithely on just the same, ignoring in practice the ridiculousness which they admit in theory, and drawing renewed hope and conceit from some magic, exhaustless source. And this is the whole philosophy of the New Year's resolution.

* * * * *

TEN.

ON THE LAST DAY OF THE YEAR

There are few people who arrive at a true understanding of life, even in the calm and disillusioned hours of reflection that come between the end of one annual period and the beginning of another. Nearly everybody has an idea at the back of his head that if only he could conquer certain difficulties and embarrassments, he might really start to live properly, in the full sense of living. And if he has pluck he says to himself: "I *will* smooth things out, and then I'll really live." In the same way, nearly everybody, regarding the spectacle of the world, sees therein a principle which he calls Evil; and he thinks: "If only we could get rid of this Evil, if only we could set things right, how splendid the world would be!" Now, in the meaning usually attached to it, there is no such positive principle as Evil. Assuming that there is such a positive principle in a given phenomenon—such as the character of a particular man—you must then admit that there is the same positive principle everywhere, for just as the character of no man is so imperfect that you could not conceive a worse, so the character of no man is so perfect that you could not conceive a better. Do away with Evil from the world, and you would not merely abolish certain specially distressing matters, you would change everything. You would in fact achieve perfection. And when we say that one thing is evil and another good, all that we mean is that one thing is less advanced than another in the way of perfection. Evil cannot therefore be a positive principle; it signifies only the falling short of perfection.

And supposing that the desires of mankind were suddenly fulfilled, and the world was rendered perfect! There would be no motive for effort, no altercation of conflicting motives in the human heart; nothing to do, no one to befriend, no anxiety, no want unsatisfied. Equilibrium would be established. A cheerful world! You can see instantly how amusing it would be. It would have only one drawback—that of being dead. Its reason for being alive would have ceased to operate. Life means change through constant development. But you cannot develop the perfect. The perfect can merely expire.

That average successful man whom I have previously cited feels all this by instinct, though he does not comprehend it by reason. He reaches his ambition, and retires from the fight in order to enjoy life,—and what does he then do? He immediately creates for himself a new series of difficulties and embarrassments, either by undertaking the management of a large estate, or by some other device. If he does not maintain for himself conditions which necessitate some kind of struggle, he quickly dies—spiritually or physically, often both. The proportion of men who, having established an equilibrium, proceed to die on the spot, is enormous. Continual effort, which means, of course, continual disappointment, is the *sine qua non*—without it there is literally nothing vital. Its abolition is the abolition of life. Hence, people, who, failing to savour the struggle itself, anticipate the end of the struggle as the beginning of joy and happiness—these people are simply missing life; they are longing to exchange life for death. The hemlock would save them a lot of weary waiting.

* * * * *

We shall now perceive, I think, what is wrong with the assumptions of the average successful man as set forth in the previous chapter. In postulating that happiness is what one is not, he has got hold of a mischievous conception of happiness. Let him examine his conception of happiness, and he will find that it consists in the enjoyment of love and luxury, and in the freedom from enforced effort. He generally wants all three ingredients. Now passionate love does not mean happiness; it means excitement, apprehension and continually renewed desire. And affectionate love, from which the passion has faded, means something less than happiness, for, mingled with its gentle tranquility is a disturbing regret for the more fiery past. Luxury, according to the universal experience of those who have had it, has no connection whatever with happiness. And as for freedom from enforced effort, it means simply death.

Happiness as it is dreamed of cannot possibly exist save for brief periods of self-deception which are followed by terrible periods of reaction. Real, practicable happiness is due primarily not to any kind of environment, but to an inward state of mind. Real happiness consists first in acceptance of the fact that discontent is a condition of life, and, second, in an honest endeavour to adjust conduct to an ideal. Real happiness is not an affair of the future; it is an affair of the present. Such as it is, if it cannot be obtained now, it can never be obtained. Real happiness lives in patience, having comprehended that if very little is accomplished towards perfection, so a man's existence is a very little moment in the vast expanse of the universal life, and having also comprehended that it is the struggle which is vital, and that the end of the struggle is only another name for death.

* * * * *

"Well," I hear you exclaiming, "if this is all we can look forward to, if this is all that real, practicable happiness amounts to, is life worth living?" That is a question which each person has to answer for himself. If he answers it in the negative, no argument, no persuasion, no sentimentalisation of the facts of life, will make him alter his opinion. Most people, however, answer it in the affirmative. Despite all the drawbacks, despite all the endless disappointments, they decide that life is worth living. There are two species of phenomena which bring them to this view. The first may be called the golden moments of life, which seem somehow in their transient brevity to atone for the dull exasperation of interminable mediocre hours: moments of triumph in the struggle, moments of fierce exultant resolve; moments of joy in nature—moments which defy oblivion in the memory, and which, being priceless, cannot be too dearly bought.

The second species of compensatory phenomena are all the agreeable experiences connected with human friendship; the general feeling, under diverse forms, that one is not alone in the world. It is for the multiplication and intensification of these phenomena that Christmas, the Feast of St. Friend, exists. And, on the last day of the year, on the eve of a renewed effort, our thoughts may profitably be centered upon a plan of campaign whose execution shall result in a less imperfect intercourse.

Lightning Source UK Ltd.
Milton Keynes UK
UKHW022329060223
416579UK00001B/166